He cupp[illegible] brilliant blue eyes shining in the dim cave. "I'm not going to let anything happen to you. You know that, right?" His voice was low, tender.

Before Abigail could respond, the strange sound seeped into the air and began to grow.

Spike grabbed her hand and broke into a dead run. "Sandstorm!"

She put everything she had into it, her lungs burning, but she wasn't fast enough. The sandstorm was upon them in minutes, blinding them, pelting their faces. Spike pulled her forward and after an eternity, they reached a gap in a nearby cliff. The crevice was barely big enough for both of them, and she practically sat on his lap.

"How long do you think it'll last?" Abigail gasped out.

"No telling. Could be hours or days." He bit out a curse. "I'd hoped we'd be able to put some distance between us and the rebels tonight." He shrugged. "For now, relax," he said, too close to her ear.

Relax? "I'm having a little trouble relaxing," she snapped at him.

They were stuck in the desert with nothing but a gallon of water and a pack of armed terrorists breathing down their backs!

Dear Harlequin Intrigue Reader,

As we ring in a new year, we have another great month of mystery and suspense coupled with steamy passion.

Here are some juicy highlights from our six-book lineup:

- Julie Miller launches a new series, THE PRECINCT, beginning with *Partner-Protector.* These books revolve around the rugged Fourth Precinct lawmen of Kansas City whom you first fell in love with in the TAYLOR CLAN series!
- *Rocky Mountain Mystery* marks the beginning of Cassie Miles's riveting new trilogy, COLORADO CRIME CONSULTANTS, about a network of private citizens who volunteer their expertise in solving criminal investigations.
- Those popular TOP SECRET BABIES return to our lineup for the next *four* months!
- Gothic-inspired tales continue in our spine-tingling ECLIPSE promotion.

And don't forget to look for Debra Webb's special Signature Spotlight title this month: *Dying To Play.*

Hopefully we've whetted your appetite for January's thrilling lineup. And be sure to check back every month to satisfy your craving for outstanding suspense reading.

Enjoy!

Denise O'Sullivan
Senior Editor
Harlequin Intrigue

SECRET SOLDIER

DANA MARTON

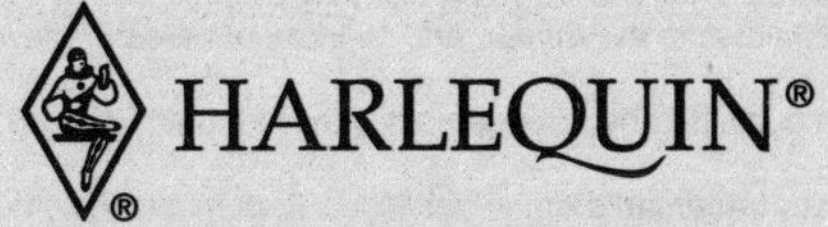

TORONTO • NEW YORK • LONDON
AMSTERDAM • PARIS • SYDNEY • HAMBURG
STOCKHOLM • ATHENS • TOKYO • MILAN • MADRID
PRAGUE • WARSAW • BUDAPEST • AUCKLAND

To Jenel and Anita. Your friendship has been such a blessing in my life. Thank you.

Acknowledgments
With many thanks to Kim Nadelson
for all her guidance, patience and kindness.

ISBN 0-373-22821-X

SECRET SOLDIER

This edition published by arrangement with Harlequin Books S.A.

www.eHarlequin.com

Printed in U.S.A.

ABOUT THE AUTHOR

Dana Marton lives near Wilmington, Delaware, and is married to her very own soldier hero. She has been an avid reader since childhood and has a master's degree in writing popular fiction. When not writing, she can be found either in her large garden or her home library.

She would love to hear from her readers via e-mail at DanaMarton@yahoo.com, or your can send post mail to: Dana Marton, P.O. Box 7987, Newark, DE 19714. SASE appreciated.

Books by Dana Marton

HARLEQUIN INTRIGUE

806—SHADOW SOLDIER
821—SECRET SOLDIER

CAST OF CHARACTERS

Dr. Abigail DiMatteo—Working hard to help war orphans in Beharrain, Abigail is more than annoyed when documentary cameraman Gerald Thornton gets in her way. Before she knows it, Abigail is chased across the desert by men hell-bent on killing her, and Gerald seems to be her only hope of getting out alive....

Jack (Spike) Logan—Member of a top secret military group (SDDU). When he is sent to Beharrain to do damage control for the CIA, under the alias of Gerald Thornton, he expects it to be a routine mission. Then he meets Dr. DiMatteo, the woman he is supposed to turn into a spy.

Colonel Wilson—Spike's boss. He's the leader of the SDDU, reporting straight to the Homeland Security Secretary.

SDDU—Special Designation Defense Unit. A top secret military team established to fight terrorism, its existence is known only by a select few. Members are recruited from the best of the best.

Suhaib Hareb—The youngest son of a prominent family in Beharrain. He is believed by the CIA to be El Jafar, the head of a new terrorist group that is planning a large scale attack against the United States.

Jamal Hareb—Suhaib's oldest brother, the family's patriarch. He is pro-reform, trying to change his country for the better. But can he be trusted?

Tsernyakov—An elusive arms dealer, wanted on three continents. Although results of his work are well-known to the authorities, his identity isn't. He is quickly working his way to the top of the international most wanted list.

Chapter One

Jack "Spike" Logan crouched behind the counter, his finger on the trigger. He couldn't hear them, but he knew they were out there somewhere in the cold night, waiting to take him down.

They were welcome to try.

He scanned the kitchen and its three possible points of entry: living room, laundry room and back porch. Too many. He kept in the cover of the counter as he crept toward the sliding glass doors.

Something rustled the azalea bush behind the swing set outside.

Not the wind. The trees and other plants in the backyard remained still, outlined against the background by the waning moon.

Somebody behind that bush was waiting to kill him. He could have shot the man from where he stood, but the sound of gunfire would have brought the other two running. He had already neutralized the rest of the twelve who'd gotten the unfortunate assignment to take him out. Still, three assailants were plenty to set a tidy trap. The man in the bush could be a decoy. Spike lifted his finger from the trigger. He needed a plan.

Careful to keep out of the patches of moonlight that illuminated the kitchen, he moved back toward the living room and waited to make sure it was clear before he entered.

The line of narrow windows looked out onto the backyard, but dense hemlocks blocked the view. Millimeter by millimeter, he pushed up one of the panels. Cold wind slammed into his face as he stuck his head out far enough to make sure no surprises waited for him in the two-foot gap between the row of hemlocks and the house. Nobody there. He should be able to get out without touching the trees and giving himself away. But first, back to the kitchen to wait.

Five minutes crawled by before the azalea bush moved again. Good, the bastard was still there. Jack lifted his gun, nice and slow, no sudden movements that might catch the other man's attention. The attacker had to be either in a crouch or lying on his stomach, facing the house. In his mind, Spike mapped the likely locations for all the vital organs. He squeezed off six shots in quick succession then dropped to the floor and rolled. No return fire. He didn't get up until he was in the living room. He made it halfway to the window when one of the two remaining men popped up outside, grabbed the sill and vaulted in.

Spike shot the guy in the middle of the chest, the hit

confirmed by the red patch that immediately bloomed on the man's bodysuit. He heard a faint scraping noise but couldn't tell from what direction it came. Since the man he'd just shot came in the back, he figured the other one would break in through the front. Spike shoved the man out of the way and jumped through the window, landing softly on the mulched ground. And the next second felt the cold metal of a gun in the back of his head.

Rodriguez. He didn't have to turn to know who it was. There was only one man on that team who could hope to come close enough to touch him. And nobody but Rodriguez was cocky enough not to take a shot when he had the chance, but think he could bring in Spike alive.

He put his hands in the air as he straightened, looking for the slightest opportunity. And it came, as it always did for those who were ready. The gun wavered slightly against his skin as the man behind him shifted. Spike dropped and threw his body weight against him, and shot him twice in the heart before they hit the ground.

"Get off me." Rodriguez swore in Spanish. "My beeper went off."

"What the hell are you talking about?" It had to be a trick. What was Rodriguez hoping for? The computerized grid built into the man's training suit had already registered the fatal hit and signaled it with the red fluorescent circle.

"It's Nicola, you idiot. I've gotta go."

Spike rolled off him and squeezed between two hemlocks to get to the open yard from the narrow spot behind the trees. "I took you fair and— Nicola?"

"The baby is coming." Rodriguez pushed through the branches, grinning like an idiot. "I've gotta run," he said and hauled ass at combat speed.

Spike stared after him, stunned to speechlessness. Alejandro Jesus Rodriguez, one of the most dangerous and toughest men he knew, one of the very few he actually respected. And the woman had him on a beeper.

It couldn't be happening. Not to a man like Rodriguez.

And yet it had.

Spike brushed off the front of his full bodysuit, free of red circles, as if what Alex had was catching. *Hell, no.* That was never going to happen to him. He shook his head and watched the rest of the team come in.

"What's wrong with Rodriguez?" The special agent who had organized the testing on the PLT suit—Precision Laser Technology—came around the corner.

"His wife is having a baby."

"No kidding? Her first? What's the rush? She'll be at it for a while. First time around, takes forever and a day."

"Yes, sir." Spike looked at the ground trying to think of something to say to change the conversation, which didn't seem fitting for an FBI training course.

"He must have had a beeper." The man sounded nostalgic.

Did this kind of thing happen all the time? Spike stepped back, not wanting to breach this previously unknown territory. Better to stay ignorant. He didn't want to know if men out there jumped and ran to commands beeped from their wives. He might never again be able to enjoy his freedom with the knowledge of such atrocities on fellow members of his gender.

"Let's go inside, then, and have a quick evaluation." Special Agent Mullock, one of a handful of men at the FBI who was aware of the SDDU's existence, pointed toward the house now that all eleven of Alex's team had arrived. "Please don't reset your suits until I confirm that the computer made an accurate recording."

Spike grunted. Nobody seemed to care that it was two o'clock in the morning. The cold front coming in all the way from Canada tried its best to freeze his balls off in the thin PLT training suit, clearly designed for fair-weather exercises. He didn't remember the last time temperatures had been this low in September. Of course, the trainees were eager to prove they were tough enough for the SDDU, Special Designation Defense Unit, America's secret weapon against terrorism. And Agent Mullock was probably too excited about testing PLT's latest wonder to think of something as mundane as the comfort of Spike's testicles.

No, that wasn't fair. Evaluating an operation was most efficient and productive if done as soon as possible afterward, while all events were most clear in the participants' heads. Spike took a deep breath and followed after the men who filed into the house through the sliding glass doors.

He partially unzipped the top of the training suit, pulled his cell phone from his T-shirt's front pocket and turned it on. Message from Colonel Wilson, received half an hour ago. "Call me at the office."

Didn't anybody sleep anymore?

He stepped back outside, punched the numbers.

The Colonel picked up on the first ring. "Where have you been?"

"FBI training course. We were testing the new PLT suits."

"I didn't know you did training."

"As a favor to Rodriguez, sir. He asked me to be the target for his new team."

A moment of silence, then, "How do you feel about doing some damage control for the CIA?"

"I can be in your office in fifteen."

"Go straight to Andrews. We have a plane waiting to take you to Beharrain. Everything you'll need is on board. An agent will fill you in on the details on the way over."

"Is it a joint operation?"

"You'll be one of multiple simultaneous efforts, but working alone. They're having trouble with a new terrorist group that's trying to make a name by executing a large-scale attack in the U.S. A couple of dates popped up in the chatter. We've got about two weeks to stop them."

"But I'll be reporting to you?" Spike asked just to be sure.

"Correct. I will be your sole point of contact."

Good. He preferred it that way. He was ready for some action and hoped the assignment to the Middle East was a good one. It had to be something unusual. The CIA didn't come around to ask the SDDU for help every day. There had to be more to the story. "You said damage control?"

"They lost some woman."

HE WASN'T real. She had to be hallucinating. Another heatstroke. Great. Dr. Abigail DiMatteo gaped at the stranger coming out of her mud hut, forgetting about the headache she'd gotten from her mother's nagging. She felt her forehead—sweaty, but not feverish. She pinched the skin on the back of her hand, and it snapped back as soon as she let it go, rather than smoothing out slowly as when people were severely dehydrated. Phew. No heatstroke. Excellent. She hated the puking.

The man, about the same height as her hut, walked to his Jeep, surrounded by more children than she'd thought lived in the village, and grabbed a load of bags then disappeared behind the worn length of fabric that served as her door. If he was an inch wider in the shoulders he would have had to go in sideways.

Who on earth was that?

She craned her neck as the truck she was riding in flew over the road toward the square—the largest common area around, and the starting and arrival point for the weekly shuttle to the market.

She willed her bones to keep from rattling apart as the truck bounced over the uneven ground. The rest of the passengers didn't seem to mind. The platform of the old Russian-made Kamaz was filled to capacity with men, women and children who had gone into Rahmara for the weekly market. They looked like some raga-muffin paramilitary group, with rifle barrels glinting in the sun. No man left the village without his gun, and weapons were in abundance thanks to the recent civil war. She had seen goatherds armed better than half the soldiers who occasionally rode through the village.

The truck slowed as it reached the center of the shantytown built on the ruins of Tukatar, a once-prosperous village destroyed by six years of war. The driver brought the vehicle to a halt, gears screeching to high heaven, and Abigail lifted her large bundle onto her back, as eager to get home as the rest of the people jumping to the sand.

Home. It was the first time she had thought of her mud hut as such since she had arrived four days ago. Amazing how a death-defying trip across the desert could make you appreciate what you had.

Home indeed. With a mysterious visitor. She walked as briskly as she could, considering the heat and the load on her back. She hadn't expected anyone. The man couldn't have looked more out of place if he tried. Tall, blond and well-built, the all-American poster boy. But he must have been at least somewhat familiar with the culture since he wore long pants instead of shorts, and a simple white shirt—nothing to offend. Despite the clothing usually thought excessive by westerners for hundred-plus degrees of heat, he didn't look like he was breaking a sweat.

She, on the other hand, was baking under the long black *abayah* she'd chosen to wear out of respect for the local customs. The veil that covered her head kept the dust out of her hair, but her face had half a pound of sand stuck to it, and her body was drenched in sweat. She couldn't remember the last time she'd been more in need of a bath. And, of course, there was no chance of that whatsoever. She barely had enough water at the hut to drink.

Her bundle of wooden bowls, sacks of flour, a jar of honey and other essentials, weighed more by the minute. But they were things she needed, things unavailable in the small village. She could get milk, cheese, eggs, fruits and vegetables from her neighbors, but for anything beyond that she had to go to town. The villagers had scarcely enough to eat after two years of drought—rarely any surplus to sell.

Tired to the bone, she shifted her load to the other shoulder. She was having a really rotten day, not in the mood for visitors at all. He'd better have brought food and some articles of comfort.

She didn't want to have to go into Rahmara for a while. Although seeing a bigger town had been interesting, the trip was murder. And she had felt compelled to call her mother as long as she was near the only phone for a hundred miles around. And her mother never missed an occasion to drive her crazy.

Abigail adjusted the bundle on her back. Next week when she went into Rahmara, she would buy a goat. She had tried to buy one from a farmer in town as soon as she'd arrived, but he refused. Probably because she was a woman. Rahmara was bigger, not as backward as Tukatar. Tukatar was strictly under the thumb of the local mullah.

The mullah. *Oh, my God!* She broke into a run. Had the village's religious leader decided to give her hut to someone else? He hadn't liked the idea of her project from the beginning and had let her stay only because of the money.

She slowed as she got closer to her hut, tried to catch her breath. The Jeep was still there. The children greeted her in a chorus, none with a wider smile than Zaki, a seven-year-old ragamuffin who'd lost his left leg in a land-mine accident.

The man was nowhere in sight.

"Hello," she called out.

No response.

Well. She didn't have to wait for acknowledgement. As far as she knew, it was still *her* home. She pulled aside the cloth that served as a door and marched right in.

"Hi." The intruder stopped unpacking and came toward her with his right hand extended, his handsome face splitting into a wide smile that revealed movie-star-quality sparkling teeth.

He overwhelmed her in every way: his size, his good looks, his incredible blue eyes. He looked somewhat swarthier up close, his face covered by the beginnings of a beard, a shade or two darker than his hair. And yet, even that could not detract from the perfect lines of his strong, masculine face. His smile radiated charisma, as his body radiated power.

"I'm Gerald Thornton from the Barnsley Foundation."

Her annoyance at a stranger making himself at home in her hut evaporated as fast as water from desert sand. He was bringing money that would save countless orphans. She lowered her bundle onto the already cluttered dirt floor and shook his hand, twice as large as her own, feeling swallowed up both by his presence and his touch. She pulled back abruptly and looked away, then back at his confident smile, trying to figure out what about him made her feel skittish. It wasn't like her to be so easily intimidated. *Ignore the man, focus on the business.*

"Does that mean I received the grant?" She drew up her eyebrows, trying to act surprised. No sense getting Lilly into trouble by letting on that her friend had leaked the news weeks ago.

His smile widened, his tanned face crinkling into laugh lines around his vibrant blue eyes and super masculine mouth. "You've got it. Congratulations!"

"Thank you. I'm stunned. And thank you for coming all this way." She certainly hadn't expected that.

"No trouble at all, Dr. DiMatteo. Bringing good news is always a pleasure."

She liked his voice. Not the kind of deep baritone that resonated in the chest, like Anthony's, the voice she had fallen in love with so much that she had ignored the rest for too long. Gerald's tone was friendly, straightforward, with a hint of smile in it. It matched the ever-present grin on his face. He was the most handsome man she'd ever met, despite the beginnings of a beard. She'd never been attracted to facial hair, but on him it looked good—gave him a little edge.

She wanted to ask him how many days he was staying, whether he could drive her to Rahmara to the bank to deposit the check so she wouldn't have to wait until next week's market to take the truck to town. But since he had just gotten there, it seemed rude to ask when he would be leaving. He had to be exhausted from the trip from New York City.

"Do you normally deliver the awards? I was under the impression I'd be notified by phone." She had checked her voice mail at home from Rahmara, but there were no messages from the foundation.

He unzipped a black leather case and pulled out a camera. "I'm going to record your entire adventure. For promotional purposes." The smile he flashed her was lethal.

She barely noticed. The words *entire adventure* echoed in her head and revived her forgotten headache. He was going to stay with her indefinitely? The ten-by-ten mud hut seemed to close in on her. She should have known the whole thing was too good to be true. No such thing as a free lunch.

He couldn't stay. She had plenty of things to do. Her project of rehabilitating war orphans was barely off the ground. No time to baby-sit some city boy. And he was a real charmer—just what she didn't need. If he as much as looked at a woman in the village, they'd both be kicked out. Or worse. What she needed was to come up with a nice polite way to say no.

"Listen, mind if I crash?" He flashed her a disarming smile that would have been enough to give any woman palpitations. "Jet lag is catching up with me."

She flushed with embarrassment. He'd caught her so off guard, she'd forgotten even the most basic courtesies. Hadn't even offered him a glass of water yet. Inconvenience or not, he had traveled halfway around the world to reach her. "Would you like a drink or something to eat?"

"Thanks. I think I'm okay for now. More tired than anything." He settled onto his sleeping bag with fluid, precise motions.

He was well-built, handsome as sin, with that larger-than-life quality of rock stars. He definitely looked as if he belonged in front of the camera rather than behind it. What an earth was she going to do with him?

"Good night, then." She tried to adjust to the thought

of him sleeping within arm's reach to her. Right. That would take more than a few seconds.

She stepped outside, needing a little distance, and watched the kids who still seemed enamored with the Jeep. They were her number-one priority. She would deal with the man inside her hut somehow. Shouldn't be that hard to come up with an excuse that would send him back.

Zaki hobbled toward her on his makeshift crutch, stumbling as it sank into the sand but catching himself in time. The bruises on his face had faded quite a bit since she'd first seen him. Because of his disability, he'd often been more successful with begging than the others, which resulted in being beaten up regularly when the bigger boys came to take his food away. She had stopped that by making it clear that any meals she gave were contingent on no more fighting. The boys took her seriously.

Zaki smiled as he greeted her. His cheeks were filling out. She smiled back. This was what she was here to do, not pose for the camera. She would talk to the kids, discuss tasks for tomorrow, give out as much food as she could and think of a polite way to get rid of Gerald in the morning. She didn't like the idea of someone looking over her shoulder twenty-four hours a day. And her instant physical attraction to him made her like the man even less.

ABIGAIL OPENED her eyes, then closed them again against the bright light that streamed through the small windows. People were talking outside. She had slept longer than usual, having spent half the night awake, wondering about what to do with Gerald.

He was still sleeping. She sat up. Should she wake him? No rush. Might as well let him get enough rest before she told him he couldn't stay. He had a long drive and an even longer plane ride ahead of him.

Someone outside called out a greeting.

Gerald's eyes popped open and focused on her—deep mountain pools of sparkling blue crystal.

She cleared her throat. "We have visitors," she said, then stood without looking at him again.

She covered her hair before stepping outside to see who it was and what they wanted. Gerald came right behind her. They'd slept fully dressed.

The mullah stood in front of her hut with a handful of men. Probably checking out the new arrival. He'd done the same thing to her.

"*Assalamuh alaikum,*" the mullah said to Gerald, and she was about to translate the greeting—peace be upon you—when Gerald responded in fluent Arabic. Better than hers.

She struggled to catch his words as he invited the mullah into her hut and apologized that he didn't have any *qahwa* ready to offer him. No coffee meant she was definitely failing as a hostess.

The men who had come with the mullah looked over the brand-new Jeep with more reserve than the children had the day before but with just as much curiosity. None of them so much as glanced at her. She wished she could go inside and find out what was going on, but of course women did not sit in conference with the men. The best she could do was eavesdrop.

She could hear bits and pieces of the conversation, the exchanging of pleasantries, a discussion on the greatness of the Prophet Muhammad—may peace be upon him—then laments on the persistent drought. She only understood about every third word, but it was enough to get the general idea. The mullah asked if she was Gerald's wife, if they were related. Gerald told him they were working together and explained about the foundation. Then there was a heated discussion, too fast to understand, although, from the change in his tone of voice, it seemed Gerald was on the defensive.

A half hour passed by before the mullah stepped outside, followed by Gerald.

"He says we can't live together if we're not related or married."

Right. In the surprise of his arrival, she had forgotten all about that. It solved her problem just fine. Looked like the mullah was going to do her dirty work for her and kick Gerald out. Much better than if she had told him to leave. The Barnsley Foundation was giving her a substantial amount of money. No sense in stepping on any toes.

She did her best to look dismayed, and to her surprise, found that she did feel a little sorry for him. If his job was as important to him as hers was to her, he must be disappointed.

"You could probably get a place in Rahmara and come out here every couple of days to film." She could handle an hour or so a week. He could get his documentary without invading her personal space and getting on her nerves.

"That's not an option."

Flexible he was not. "You could build yourself a mud hut," she said just to spite him, but he seemed to take her seriously.

"Even if I didn't live with you, we would still be working closely together. We'd still be alone a lot."

He was right. It would be best if he left. "Maybe filming the project is not a good idea. I mean, under the circumstances. And it's bound to be a diversion, which I can scarcely afford."

"Without the Barnsley Foundation, you couldn't afford the project at all."

Would they withdraw the funds if she refused to cooperate with the documentary? Was that what he was hinting at?

Diplomacy was what she needed, not an outright confrontation. She had to show him some deference, at least until the money was in her bank account. "What do you recommend?"

"Marriage."

"Very funny."

"It will allow us to work together. We can get divorced as soon as we're back in the States. If it means saving countless children from starvation, I'm willing to do it." His piercing blue eyes pinned her down.

And of course, after that last line, she couldn't very well say *she* wasn't. Still. "I believe in the sanctity of marriage," she said, as a good Catholic girl should.

"Having a man around could make things infinitely easier for you." He flashed her a smile that was the devil's own.

He was right. Getting things done was hard almost to the point of impossible, as most men refused to talk to her due to her gender. Her project would move twice as fast with Gerald's language skills and his ability to relate to the villagers.

But she couldn't get married like this. If her mother found out, she would need resuscitation. "I'm sorry, but I can't. You will have to return."

"You don't understand. You living as a single woman on your own made the mullah nervous. You were setting a bad example, corrupting morals. He only let you stay in the first place because you told him you were bringing foreign money into the village. The more prosperous the village, the more prestige he has."

"So? I'll still bring the money. The grant is not tied to you being here, is it?" Diplomacy aside, she had to know where she stood.

"It's gone past that. He asked me if I was willing to marry you and I said yes."

"And I say no."

"Technically, you don't really get a say, although I'm prepared to respect your wishes. But if you challenge the mullah's authority like this, I doubt he'll let you stay." He looked away.

Why did she have a feeling there was more? "And?"

"You spent a night with a man who's not your husband. They can stone you for that here."

"That's ridiculous. Beharrain has a modern court system. Stoning has been illegal for years."

"In theory, yes. To make the country more acceptable to western sensibilities and attract more foreign aid. But reforms take a long time to take root, especially in outlying areas like this. In this village, the mullah's word is law, and I'm telling you, he's a *very* old-fashioned man."

Abigail stared at the dust at her feet, unwilling to look at the two men who had so swiftly arranged her fate. She didn't want to get married. She especially didn't want to get married to pretty-boy Gerald Thornton. But staying single wasn't her main objective. Saving children was. And if she had to sacrifice some personal preferences to achieve her goals, then so be it. It was temporary.

"Fine," she said. "Can he marry us?"

"Probably not. We're not Muslims. But he wants it done before nightfall."

"Great. And wouldn't you know it, there's not a priest in sight."

"I bet the U.S. Embassy at Rahmara has a justice of the peace."

The man seemed to have an answer for everything, didn't he? She gave him the evil eye, but nodded.

Gerald translated for the mullah and the man responded at length, speaking too rapidly for her to understand.

"What did he say?"

"He's going to get one of the village elders to come with us as a witness and his widowed sister as your chaperone."

For crying out loud. She seethed in silence as Gerald and the mullah said their ceremonial goodbyes. Unbelievable. She backed away, into the sanctuary of her hut. How did this happen? Her life had turned beyond ridiculous in a blink of an eye. Thanks to Gerald Thornton. She sank to her mattress, unable to think; then, after a moment, she stood again. She couldn't afford to fall apart.

She had to get ready for her wedding.

"I DO," Spike said, grateful that they weren't really getting married, that the woman next to him was pledging eternal love and faithfulness to Gerald Thornton, a man who didn't exist outside a fake passport.

He wasn't the marrying type and even if he were he wouldn't have chosen her. She had looked frightful when she'd walked into her hut and he'd first seen her, and cleaning up only marginally improved her appearance. Her figure remained hidden under the shapeless *abayah*, her hair under a black scarf. He caught a glimpse of it in the dim hut that morning, a nondescript brownish color, tied into a bun. The women he normally associated with were always expertly done up, from their expensive pedicures to their hairstyles and form-fitting designer clothes.

He liked feminine women, flirty and wild. Nothing wrong with that.

Except that he had just married a humorless, ordinary, goody-two-shoes academic.

Not for real. And just for a few weeks, no more. He had to keep that in mind. And in the meantime, it could work to their advantage that she was the plain-Jane type. Certainly nobody would think by looking at her that she was up to something.

The justice of the peace went on, and the witnesses, understanding not a word of the ceremony, fidgeted behind them.

"You may kiss the bride."

Spike bit back a smile at the unhappy scowl on her face. Technically, the buildings of the U.S. Embassy counted as U.S. territory, but physical contact would have been grossly offensive to their witnesses, who no doubt would have complained to the mullah. No reason to unnecessarily aggravate anyone. "We're skipping that part," he said.

He could swear he heard her sigh of relief. Which was really strange. The one constant in his life was that women responded well to him. Enthusiastically well. Except Dr. DiMatteo. She was an odd bird, hard to figure out.

The justice of the peace smiled at them. "Congratulations."

Spike shook the man's hand. "Thank you. I appreciate—" His ringing cell phone cut him off. "Excuse me." He stepped away from the small wedding party as he clicked it on. "Thornton."

"Have you made contact?" The Colonel's voice cut in and out.

"Yes." He couldn't say more than that with Abigail and the others standing a few feet from him.

"Well done. Remember the CIA's multipronged approach I told you about? Their asset turned up dead yesterday. Then this morning, they rushed the house they'd been keeping under surveillance and found it cleared out. You are it, Logan. You and Dr. DiMatteo. You need to start her evaluation immediately."

"Will do." He had begun the second he'd set eyes on her. From what he could tell so far, she was not fit for the job. She was as see-through as a fancy negligee. The idea of recruiting her for the CIA seemed worse by the minute. Definitely not undercover material. Her face showed every wayward emotion that crossed her mind. She had known that she'd gotten the grant. He'd seen it in her face and had wondered who'd tipped her off. And she had planned to send him packing, which was why he'd gone to bed early, pretending to sleep to gain time until morning.

He had counted on the mullah's vigilance and it worked. They were in a country where unrelated men and women didn't eat, work or spend any time together whatsoever. He couldn't very well evaluate, recruit and train her like that. But now they were married, and in this part of the world that meant she was under his power in every way, tied to him. He needed that to complete his mission successfully.

He had two weeks to lead the CIA to the terrorists' headquarters, probably a training camp either in the mountains or in the desert. If he failed, the U.S. military would have to come in and bomb a variety of possible targets. And since the Beharrainian government refused to give permission for any type of U.S. military operation in the country, that kind of intervention would mean out-and-out war.

And still, there would be a chance that El Jafar—aka Suhaib Hareb, the head of the terrorist group, according to CIA intelligence—could slip through somehow and succeed with his attack against the U.S.

Spike dropped the phone into his pocket. Somehow within the next two weeks, he had to find a way to pin down El Jafar. And his temporary wife was the key to the whole operation. He hoped to hell she was up for the task.

Chapter Two

"*Shukran*, El Jafar," Tsernyakov, if that was his real name, thanked him. "I will be in touch about details on transportation." He extended his hand.

They kissed on the cheek three times as was customary among friends. He allowed Tsernyakov the familiarity because he wanted him to feel safe.

"It's a good deal." The Russian smiled, visibly pleased.

An excellent deal. El Jafar watched as his guards escorted the man out of the spacious tent, but in his mind he was seeing something else—news reports of his victory.

The vivid picture in his head chased his bad mood away. He always had the ability to see clearly the things he wanted, as if they'd already happened. He was a visionary—one much needed by his people.

The first strike had to be spectacular—bigger and more devastating than the U.S.A. had ever seen. After that, once everybody knew his name, recruits would be abundant and funding would flow in. And with that, the second attack would be even better. His cause was just, and he would not stop until he brought his enemies to their knees. He could no longer argue reasonably while no one in political office listened. He could not stand by and watch as western businesses, backed by their governments, robbed and raped his country.

He was a successful businessman, but what he and his family had paled in comparison to what should have been rightfully theirs. They should have been living like princes. They would have been, if westerners had not supported King Majid's claims to the throne, ensuring his favor that came with hefty government contracts. El Jafar fisted his hand. Contracts that should have gone to his company and other local interests, not to some global conglomerate who siphoned the profits back to the West, harvesting the riches while leaving Beharrain in poverty.

Fair Trade was nothing but a slogan. If trade were fair, countries with valuable natural resources wouldn't have to watch their citizens starve while their western trade partners got richer and richer, to the point of obscenity.

But not much longer. The day of reckoning was coming soon. And the thieves would have nowhere to hide.

Tsernyakov had come through. He trusted the man, or, at least, he trusted him as much as he trusted anyone. Still, he'd been careful. He had not revealed his real name, his purpose or his location. At each meeting, he'd sent a car to pick up Tsernyakov at his hotel and drive him out into the desert. The tent, a reminder of his Bedouin ancestors, had been set up at a different place each time.

"Forgive me, El Jafar." One of his men was at the tent's opening. "Hamid begs for a word with you."

"Send him in." He smiled, pleased beyond measure with the way his plan was progressing, faster than even he had expected. In another ten days or so, the world would know his name. And his enemies would learn to fear him.

ABIGAIL GRABBED for her seat as Gerald swerved to avoid a giant pothole. She glanced at Leila next to her on the back seat. Neither she nor Abdul, riding shotgun with his rifle slung over his shoulder, seemed perturbed by the road conditions. As far as Abigail could see in the approaching twilight, their path was riddled with craters from shelling. Although the civil war had been over for almost four years, no one had the money to even begin repairs. But Gerald was proving useful at last, handling the obstacles with the agility of a race car driver.

Mrs. Gerald Thornton. She turned the words over in her head for the hundredth time since they'd left Rahmara. She was married. Just like that. She caught Gerald's gaze in the rearview mirror and he winked at her.

She bit back a groan. God, what had she done?

Their marriage was a lie and, beyond any other sin,

she hated deceit the most. She should have thought of that earlier. And, of course, she had. But she had to be practical. Their marriage hurt no one, while it made possible for her to stay in Tukatar and save children. That outweighed everything. And then, of course, there was that whole "stoning to death" issue. She hoped the locals would think twice before enforcing such a punishment on a U.S. citizen, but she hadn't been brave enough to test the mullah.

Leila, her chaperone, a short but stocky widow covered from head to toe in a black *abayah*, said something to her brother. He shrugged. Maybe she was too hot. They had the Jeep's roof up to keep the sun off them, but it didn't help much. Abigail looked down on her own identical attire, which was roasting her alive.

She'd worn black to her wedding.

It should have told anyone who cared to pay attention how she felt about this very special occasion.

She turned west, where the sun was dipping behind the mountains at last. Cool night air couldn't come fast enough, although she didn't feel all that comfortable being on the road after dark. She didn't cherish the thought of breaking her neck, or some other body part, when the Jeep hit a pothole. She kept her eyes on the road, squinting when a swirl of rising dust in the distance caught her attention. It seemed to move toward them.

"What's that?"

Gerald leaned forward. "Army trucks." He didn't seem to be worried.

Thank God, Leila and her brother had come along. Westerners were common in the bigger cities, but out in the country, mistrust of them still ran high. They were sure to be stopped, their papers examined. But at least Abdul could vouch for them. She hoped they wouldn't be held up long. Night was fast approaching.

The vehicles were close enough now to count—four open-bed army trucks, their backs filled with men. They came to a dusty halt and blocked the road. A handful of men jumped off the first vehicle, some with rifles, some with machine guns. A man got out of the cab, better dressed and better fed than the rest, wearing a military uniform, a once-white turban covering his head.

Gerald brought the Jeep to a slow stop and called out a respectful greeting.

"Get out," the man ordered in a strange dialect.

She didn't like the way he was looking at them. And she really, really didn't want to get out of the car. Not that the Jeep could save them. They might be able to outrun the trucks, but they couldn't outrun the bullets.

With unhurried motions, Gerald stepped onto the sand and moved a couple of feet away from the vehicle. She followed his example. On the other side of the car, Abdul and Leila did the same.

More men came off the trucks then, some surrounding them, some going through the Jeep. They were thin to the last man, their mismatched, worn clothes hanging on them, their scraggly beards not quite covering their hollow cheeks. Nobody asked for papers.

"Bandits," Gerald whispered.

She sucked in her breath. According to the villagers, the bandits who controlled the mountains did not come into the desert as far as the road that led to Tukatar. Had hunger forced them to stray from their territory?

She watched as the bandits unloaded the food they had purchased in town. The bundles quickly disappeared into the back of the army trucks.

The raggedy group looked hungry and wild. Not much distinguished them from the army troops that rode through the villages from time to time. The bandits stole from the army as much as from anyone else. Most of the men had at least one part of some uniform on them. Because the army could scarcely afford to keep its soldiers in new uniforms, they were also dressed in a blend of military and civilian clothing. Since provisions were scarce, even army troops were often forced to seize food and supplies from the general population.

She hoped Gerald was wrong and the small group in front of them was a renegade army unit. Soldiers might take everything, but would probably leave their lives. Bandits were more likely to massacre them and leave them for the buzzards. If they were lucky.

She listened as Abdul negotiated with the men in rapid-fire Arab. She caught enough to get the gist of the conversation.

They wanted the women.

Oh, God. She grabbed onto the back of Gerald's shirt.

"No," he said firmly.

A dozen guns were immediately aimed at them.

One of the men headed for Leila. Abdul stepped in front of her and took his rifle off his back. Everybody shouted at once, both the bandit leader and Abdul gesturing wildly. Abdul leveled his rifle, shouted something and put his finger on the trigger. The voices stopped for a moment, even the air seemed to stand still.

She realized what was going to happen about a split second before the shots rang out. She screamed, her voice drowned by the renewed yelling of the men and the sound of gunfire. It didn't seem real. When Abdul and Leila crumpled to the ground, she half expected them to get up.

The guns fell silent.

She stood frozen to the spot, unable to look away from the bodies and the sand that greedily drank in their blood. They were both dead. And Gerald and she were next.

The leader shouted at his men, clearly displeased, and ordered them to salvage whatever clothes they could from the bodies. She turned away, trembling, and caught sight of Gerald with his hands in the air. She should have done the same, except it didn't seem she had that much control over her body.

The leader of the bandits looked at her and Gerald, and walked over to them. Gerald shifted, blocking her view. It took her a few seconds to realize he was trying to shield her from the man.

"If two United States citizens disappear, soldiers will be all over your mountain," Gerald said in a calm voice and nodded toward the peaks. "You have a good camp up there, a warm cave. Winter is coming soon. Bad time to take your people on the run."

The man sneered at him, his dark eyes vivid with anger. "I own the mountain. I take what I want." He pulled his pistol from his belt and pointed it at Gerald.

Her lungs shrank; her heart slammed against her chest.

"Get on the truck." The man jerked his head toward one of the vehicles.

Gerald glanced back at her and nodded. How the hell could he stay calm at a time like this? She stared after him as he walked toward the truck, but could not follow. Her legs weren't working.

One of the bandits came over to her and shoved her roughly. She caught herself from falling and stumbled forward. Then two men grabbed her and pulled her up into the back of the truck. She scampered to the front, to Gerald, although she knew he could offer no protection. He pushed her down on the end of the wooden bench and sat next to her. One of the bandits shoved Gerald over and sat between them.

A few more men climbed up, six of them altogether in the back of the truck. They didn't look friendly. A couple worked on stretching camouflage canvas over the metal ribs that arched above. She watched them with a strange detachment, as if seeing a movie. She was pretty sure she was in shock. She'd seen the aftermath of violence before, almost more than she could handle, but had never been part of it.

Leila and Abdul were dead.

She glanced at the bodies on the sand, but then the men finally secured the canvas so she couldn't see out any longer. The sky was darkening, and the back of the truck was darker yet. Somebody yelled to them from the ground. The rushing blood in her ears drowned out the words.

One of the bandits got up, ordered Gerald to stand and patted him down, taking the cell phone from his pocket and the watch from his wrist.

"No weapons," he yelled back before sitting to look at the phone. He pushed a couple of buttons, gave a frustrated groan, slipped the thing into the front pocket of his uniform and put the watch on.

Gerald didn't say a word, which was probably the smart thing to do. And yet, she couldn't help wishing for a miracle—that he would spring up and subdue their kidnappers. Of course, it would have been impossible, even if he knew how to fight and had not gained his muscles pumping iron in front of a mirror in a gym.

The motors roared to life, startling her. Their truck lurched ahead. Panic replaced her numbness, filling her veins in a slow trickle, spreading through her limbs. She was going to die, and get gang-raped first, most likely. Her lungs struggled for air. She shouldn't have fought with her mother the day before.

Maybe Mom had been right. Maybe she should have never come here. Her family would be devastated when they received news that she had vanished. They would probably never find out what had happened to her.

Her sister's death had nearly broken their parents. Her own disappearance was sure to finish the job.

THEIR TRUCK was second to last. Spike surveyed the men. They were underfed and tired. He figured at least a good hour's ride to the foothills, then however long it would take them to get to camp. Not that he planned to allow things to go that far.

Were he alone, he would have been tempted to let them take him to their caves, talk them into holding him for ransom, stick around until he could determine whether they had any ties to the terrorists. But he wasn't alone, and he could see no positive outcome for Abigail once they reached the bandits' camp. And he didn't really have time to pursue a tenuous lead such as this, anyhow. Jamal Hareb was their best chance. They couldn't afford any detours.

He waited about twenty minutes, until the night and the rhythmic rattle of the truck over the sand soothed the men into complacency. He took a deep breath, ignoring the stench of unwashed bodies, and bent to scratch his ankle, retrieving a switchblade hidden in the sole of his ordinary-looking sandal.

He straightened and leaned back in his seat, letting his eyelids drift closed. Two of the six men were sleeping; the rest were on the brink. Without opening his eyes, he put his arm on the back of the seat, as if trying to make himself more comfortable. He struck with the next big bump in the road, barely moving his hand. The man sitting between him and Abigail slumped down in his seat with a small groan that sounded like a snort. Nobody else moved. He pulled his blade from the man's heart, mumbled as if in his sleep and turned toward his other side.

That one made more noise than the first. Spike coughed, then held his breath as he watched the man's head fall on the sleeping bandit's shoulder next to him. He didn't wake up. Nobody stirred in the near pitch dark.

Two down, four to go. He wanted to take care of the ones who were awake first. They sat side by side, across from Abigail. Spike leaned toward them.

"I have to relieve myself," he said in a voice low enough not to wake the sleepers.

"We'll be there soon enough," one of the men responded.

He leaned forward as if he hadn't caught the words. Then, before either of the men knew what was happening, he had his knife buried in the chest of one, the neck of the other broken in the crook of his arm. One of the rifles fell to the floor with a thud before he could catch it and woke the rest. Too late. He reached them in two steps.

When he was done with the last man, he picked up

one of the rifles and stepped over the bodies to get back to Abigail. "Get down."

No time to reassure her. She'd just have to deal with the situation. To her credit, she had stayed quiet the whole time and was now obeying his order, though her eyes were as round as a pair of quarters as she stared at him in shock.

He shot through the cab's back window, hitting the guy in the passenger seat first, then the driver. The truck veered sharply to the right but kept on going full speed, the dead man's foot heavy on the gas pedal.

"Hang on. Stay where you are." He pulled the canvas aside, grabbed the metal bar then climbed out.

A bullet went by so close, it moved his hair. More shots. He hoped none of them hit Abigail. He yanked the driver-side door open and pulled the man out. The truck slowed momentarily, but then he was in the seat, his feet shoved hard against the gas pedal.

Yeah, baby. He grinned; he was in his element at last and loving the challenge of it. He kept his eyes on the road, what little of it he could see by his lone headlight and the half moon above.

He managed to gain some distance from the truckload of bandits behind them, but not enough to be out of rifle range. The bandits were shooting up their vehicle as if they were in competition. And then he heard the answering shots from the back. Dr. DiMatteo was returning fire. He grinned. Excellent. She hadn't forgotten how to shoot.

He watched in his side mirror as one of the trucks stopped following, then another. She must have taken out their tires. Smart woman.

There was a gap in the shooting from the back. Did she get hit? He swore and glanced back, but couldn't see anything. Then the sound of repeat fire filled the cab. She'd managed to find the semiautomatic in the darkness.

The last truck fell back slowly. Then he could see nothing in the side mirror but darkness behind them. Still, he drove for a solid half hour before he stopped.

"Are you okay?" He jumped from his seat and ran to the back.

She was sitting on the floor among the dead bodies, her face as pale as the moon, her hands trembling. He had to climb up to help her down; he didn't think she could manage by herself.

He dumped the body from the passenger seat, helped her up, then went back to dispose of the rest of the dead. Even though he hated to waste the time, he wasn't sure she could handle a load of bodies in the back. She'd had enough of a shock for the day. He could do this one thing for her. He didn't bother to search the men, but made sure he got back his phone and watch. He also kept the guns.

She was doubled over in her seat when he came back, her face buried in her hands.

"Were you hit?"

She straightened to look at him, her face tear-streaked, and shook her head.

He let out his breath. "You did good."

He turned the truck in the general direction of Tukatar, figuring they'd find the road sooner or later. "We'll be home in another hour or so."

They weren't more than fifty-sixty miles northwest of the village.

Unfortunately, they ran out of gas in ten.

ABIGAIL LOOKED at Gerald and found him watching her. He had lost some of that polished look; his face was dirty, his shirt smudged with dried blood. She blinked. What had happened back there? How had he turned from cameraman playboy into superhero?

Obviously she knew even less about her temporary husband than she'd thought.

"You okay?" His intense blue gaze searched her face.

"Still alive." Thanks to him. But for how long? "Now what?"

"The extra cans of gas are on another truck. We walk as far as we can, then we rest."

"Will your cell phone work out here?"

"Probably not," he said, but then tried anyway. He looked at the display and shook his head. "Let's go."

She took a deep breath and looked around, shivering. She had planned on being back in her hut by now and hadn't brought anything warm. Gerald's footsteps sounded soft on the sand. She forced herself to follow him.

They walked in silence for a while, and she wondered whether the scorpions or exposure would get them first, or if the bandits would catch up with them. "Do you think we're going to make it?"

Gerald looked at her and held her gaze. "I know so."

She thought of the carnage in the back of the truck and wanted more than anything to ask him how he'd done that, but she couldn't yet bring herself to speak of it. Maybe, in addition to being a cameraman, he was also a self-defense expert. Or maybe he was a spy. No, that was stupid. Why on earth would he be interested in Tukatar? People there barely had enough resources to survive, let alone conspire against anyone.

And yet something about him didn't add up. He was a cameraman from New York. Well-built, definitely a jock, probably a health club addict. But that didn't explain how he knew how to disarm and annihilate a truckful of armed men. She didn't think stuff like that could happen outside of Steven Seagal movies. There was more to Gerald Thornton than met the eye. For one, there had been no mention of a documentary in any of the grant information. Of course, they could have come up with it later. Or not.

But on the off chance that he *was* some kind of a spy, confronting him with her theories in the middle of the desert hardly seemed the smartest thing to do. He could get upset that his cover was blown and could just leave her there. Maybe he was part of a spy ring trying to set up in Beharrain, working on establishing a believable cover, getting ready for some future operation. What that operation could possibly be, she couldn't fathom. The country was poor beyond measure, sick and tired of war. She had trouble believing it would present a threat to anyone.

Abigail pushed her doubts about Gerald out of her mind. She could always ask him later. Right now, she had more important things to worry about—surviving to the next day, for one.

She glanced over her shoulder at the road behind them. Empty. Their chance for a speedy rescue was a nice fat zero. Nobody in Tukatar owned a vehicle and it wasn't market day. The truck wouldn't come again until next Wednesday, five days from now. And the bandits were still out there, probably tracking them.

Tufts of dry grasses broke up the sand here and there, and the few trees she could see were scraggly, without a single leaf. It looked as though in better years there had been enough water running off the hills to support vegetation. Since then, however, the sand had established a firm hold as far as the eye could see.

Walking on the uneven ground was difficult, the road not much more than a couple of tire tracks snaking toward the horizon. If the wind rose and the slightest sand storm kicked up, they'd be lost in the desert forever.

She tripped on the *abayah*, but Gerald caught her. The man had good reflexes.

"Tell me what you've done since you got here." He was moving forward at an even pace.

She stared after him. Back in reporter mode? Maybe

that was all he was. She hurried to catch up. Still, how on earth could he think about gathering material for his documentary at a time like this? Then again, thinking about anything but the distinct possibility of a slow death under the scorching sun—provided they survived the night—was an improvement.

She had a hard time arranging her thoughts. "Right now, I'm trying to establish credibility." Without that, she could accomplish nothing. "Respect the customs, make no waves, prove that I'm not here to pass judgment or change their ways."

"I liked your ideas on community building," he said, surprising her.

He'd read her grant proposal.

"Wars destroy more than lives. And civil war is worse. It takes everything—security, sense of identity, pride, trust. It's not like when people band together to fight an outside enemy. Civil war is about brother fighting against brother. It takes society apart at a very basic level."

"How many kids did you get to participate in your program so far?"

"Twelve boys." Pathetically few, considering the UN put the number of displaced children at around twelve thousand just in this corner of the country.

"No girls?"

She shook her head. "They're more likely to be adopted by relatives. Most of them are married off at an early age anyway and can help with work around the house until then. They inherit no property."

"Less trouble."

"I suppose," she said and thought about the rumors of young homeless girls being abducted from the streets of larger towns and being sold as servants or prostitutes. "There's much to be done."

"You've made a good start."

"Right now, the boys pretty much come to me only for the free food, but hopefully that'll change. I'm teaching them the alphabet one letter at a time with each meal."

"You're giving them a future."

God, she hoped so. But to get there, first they needed to survive the present. "I'm trying to work with some of the locals. Talk the boys into working for them for free. Dig fields, build huts, carve bowls, whatever. If the boys damage anything, I'll pay for it."

"So the boys would learn some usable skills," he said, surprising her by how fast he got the idea.

"And change the perception of the village. Most people think of them as beggars and thieves. That's still true. After all, it's hard to be a law-abiding citizen when you're starving to death. But I'm trying to change that."

"And if a farmer or butcher or whoever produces more because of the extra help, eventually they'll be able to pay the boys, in trade if nothing else."

She nodded. "That's the plan."

"Is it working?"

"We just began. A couple of boys are helping someone to put up a new mud hut. They've been making and drying mud bricks. I think the hut will be going up today. Once they learn how to do that, I'm hoping to talk them into showing the rest how it's done. If they could build some kind of shelter, they'd be off the streets. They'd have something."

"They'd have a hell of a lot. Some of their pride back, for starters."

He sounded impressed, and she couldn't deny it felt good.

The next thing she knew, her right foot sank into the sand up to her knee and she was in excruciating pain, her ankle twisted. She'd stepped into a hole, created either by some burrowing animal or a sand drift.

Gerald pulled her up. She plopped to the ground, unable to put any weight on that foot. Great. She was smart enough to know when she was screwed.

"Are you okay?" Gerald squatted in front of her, his concern obvious on his face.

The only thing she could think to say was "Go on, save yourself," but it seemed too melodramatic to actually say aloud.

"How far do you think we are?" she asked, knowing that it didn't really matter. She couldn't have made it if Tukatar was around the next tall dune.

"I figure we'll be within sight of the village by noon."

He would be. Not her. Another twelve hours of walking was out of the question. "Hurry back."

"I'm not leaving you."

"Then we both die." It wasn't unusual for the temperature to be well over ninety by nine o'clock in the morning. She hoped she'd be too loopy from sunstroke by the end to know what was going on. "Go."

Chapter Three

Spike stared at her. She was too quick to give up on herself, as if she didn't think she was worth the fight. He wondered who the hell had given her that idea. She didn't give up on others; that was clear from the way she'd been talking about the boys.

He pulled up her *abayah* and pushed her pant leg out of the way to take a look at her ankle. Not that he could see all that much in the moonlight. He felt the bones, the muscles. "Nothing feels broken. It's probably a sprain."

She had slim ankles and incredibly smooth skin—and now was definitely not the right time to notice it. He pulled back and turned around. "Hop on."

She didn't move.

"Let's not waste time with arguing." He bent his knees, relieved when she pushed herself up.

Her arms came around his neck. He put out his hands, and she put her right leg up, then the left. He adjusted her weight, keeping her legs wrapped securely around his waist from behind. "We'll be there before you know it." He started off at a good pace.

She weighed next to nothing. He'd run miles with heavier equipment than her during his training. Which brought her training to mind. Was she a suitable recruit? That was what he needed to think about, instead of how her body felt pressed against his. He had to focus on evaluating her skills, not her curves.

She didn't panic at the sight of the bandits and she toughed it out when she was hurt. She was a crack shot according to the CIA profile he'd read on the plane over here, and her performance with the guns had certainly proven that. She'd been on her university biathlon team, one of the best.

She wasn't a hopeless candidate, but neither was she a good one. She couldn't keep a secret if she tried. Not that she would talk, but her expressive face betrayed her emotions all too easily. She didn't look tough enough for the job, but that could be a plus. She wouldn't look tough enough to the enemy, either. And the fact that she was a woman might work to her advantage. In a country where women were thought capable of little, she probably wouldn't be suspected as an undercover CIA operative.

And that was what he was supposed to turn her into, despite all the things she didn't have to be a perfect fit for the job. Because she had something nobody else did—she had gone to college with Jamal Hareb, the oldest son of a prominent Beharrainian family whose youngest son, Suhaib Hareb, aka El Jafar, was suspected of heading a relatively new terrorist organization. A group who, according to intelligence, sought to make a name for itself by orchestrating a massive attack against the United States.

The plan had been simple. The CIA had fixed the grant competition so Abigail would be the winner. They were going to evaluate her and, if she passed, train her. She was suppose to "run into" Jamal, a woman alone in a foreign country—as non-threatening as they come—and somehow gain an invitation into the family home, observe what she could, plant a couple of bugs and get out. The family claimed they had cut off relations with their youngest son years ago. The CIA wasn't buying it.

Their plan was workable, if a long shot. Except that Abigail had taken off for Beharrain before the grant allocations were announced, before the CIA had gotten their act together enough to make contact. Now here he was, trying to do last-minute damage control.

He shifted her weight again. If she was hurting, she gave no sign of it. She was tough, he had to give her that. But for this job, toughness wasn't the only thing required. If all went well, she wouldn't need that or her skills with the gun. All she had to do was to place the bugs and walk away before all hell broke loose. Mental, more than physical, toughness was what she needed, the ability to play a convincing role without becoming frazzled. The question was, could she do it?

His phone buzzed in his pocket. If her leg weren't right on it, he would have ignored it. He didn't want to have to explain how he came to have superspy equipment that worked even in impossible places like the middle of the desert, which is why he had lied about it earlier when she'd asked.

"We must be just in the right spot, with the right communication satellite passing over." He got the phone and wedged it between his shoulders and ear without stopping to put her down.

"Thornton."

"Our target acquired enriched uranium yesterday," the colonel said without wasting any time on pleasantries. "He could have a dirty bomb within days. You have to move fast."

"Will do." But what about Abigail? Was there time to ditch her and come up with a different cover for him?

"Our friends at the agency would prefer if she didn't know anything," the colonel said as if he'd read his mind. "No time to give her proper training. We can't risk that she'll blow the operation. You'll have to take care of things now. Her friend is visiting one of the family companies in Tihrin this week. You must make contact within forty-eight hours at the latest. Use her to get in, then do what has to be done."

The colonel clicked off.

"You won't believe this, but we're stuck in the desert on the road between Rahmara and Tukatar.... Yeah. Bandits. Listen, my battery is going. I'd appreciate if you could give a call to the police at Rahmara to come and pick us up. Thanks, I—" He pulled the phone away from his ear and slipped it back into his pocket. "Battery's dead," he said for Abigail's benefit.

"Who was that?"

"My boss."

"Should we stop and wait for the police to come and get us?" Her hot breath tickled his ear from behind.

"Better keep on going. I'd prefer to be as far from those mountains and the bandits as possible."

"Of course," she said with a sigh that pressed her breasts against his back.

A quick bolt of heat shot through his gut, causing his step to falter. Whoa. He squelched the unexpected sensation and forced his mind to his mission. He couldn't afford to let her grow into a distraction. Being saddled with an untrained civilian in the middle of a top-secret military operation was difficult enough.

He would have preferred to leave Abigail at Tukatar and then go to take care of this business on his own. But that was the CIA for you. Not only did they tell you what to do, but they also told you exactly how to do it and then blamed you if anything went wrong. Precisely why he was in the SDDU instead. And yet, he'd managed to land in the middle of this mess.

He had to use Abigail without her knowing. Not that it would be that hard, but he hated doing it. She hadn't signed up for this. What right did he have to risk her life?

He could think of no way to talk her into going to

Tihrin with him and willingly abandon her project. Which meant he had to make it impossible for her to remain in Tukatar.

Tomorrow at the latest.

ABIGAIL SQUINTED, half-blind from the sun, her arms sore from hanging on to Gerald's shoulders for hours. He had a slim waist. Her legs were wrapped around it. She tried not to be too frazzled by that, or by the solid muscles pressed against her.

"Are you okay?" Gerald turned his head sideways and his stubble-covered cheek collided with her nose.

She pulled back. "Fine."

"Let's rest a few minutes." He headed toward a baby palm tree, no more than nine feet tall, a hundred yards or so from the road.

"Sounds good." He probably needed a break. She hated being a burden.

"Keep hanging on to me," he said when they reached the tree and he let her good leg down first then the injured one.

Pain shot up her ankle as soon as her foot touched the sand.

He reached for her arm, turned around to face her. "How does it feel?"

"Okay." She stood on one leg, which had long ago gone to sleep, hoping he wouldn't step away and let her fall face-first into the sand.

He didn't look like he was going anywhere. He

watched her with that intensity that rarely left his eyes, and she got the distinct feeling he was trying to make some kind of a decision. Maybe he had finally realized how much better off he would be if he left her.

She tried to put weight on her right foot again, but couldn't. "Still not working." She owed him the truth.

"I'll take care of it when we get back to Tukatar. You just need rest and a cold compress. It'll be as good as new in a day or two."

He sounded very sure of himself. Like Anthony always had. That had been what attracted her to Anthony in the first place. It was nice to be with someone who wasn't riddled with self-doubt all the time as she was. And, of course, he was very handsome, and very charming, and very Italian, which guaranteed her parents' unconditional approval.

"Let's sit." Gerald lowered her gently to the sand.

Sitting felt good. She rolled her neck. The sun was up. They had walked all night, but still the hardest part of their journey was ahead of them. From now on, they would be walking in increasing heat.

Gerald turned his attention to the tree, and she relaxed a little. He had a way of unnerving her. His body was imposing, for sure. But more than that, he had a kind of infectious charisma that drew her in. And she did not want to be drawn to him. She didn't even want to like him. He was a pain in the butt, interfering with her work. She should have turned him around and sent him packing the minute he had arrived.

Not that he was that terrible. She hardly knew him enough to make judgments about his character. What she didn't like was the instant attraction she felt for him. Physical attraction. Which, she knew from experience, meant absolutely nothing. Nil. It served only to confuse people and distract them from more important issues.

She didn't want to be attracted to a stranger—a coworker, really. The fact that he was her temporary husband made things even worse. Marriage or a long-term relationship was not in the cards for her, she was pretty sure of that. Her life was too crazy. And she wasn't the type for casual affairs. She longed for more. But more she couldn't have. Not with the life she had chosen to live. Who in his right mind would understand, let alone want to share this with her?

She glanced around at the endless desert to the east, at the mountains behind them. The bandits were out there somewhere. But so were the kids who needed her. Whatever happened, she was glad she had come.

"Thirsty?" Gerald was eyeing the date palm, knife in hand.

She was so dry her tongue was sticking to the roof of her mouth. "It's not nice to tease."

He grinned and sliced into a lower branch near its base. A clear liquid oozed from the cut. "Sap. Come on." He reached out his hand to her.

She grabbed on. "You first." He had carried her for hours. He needed it more.

"Don't worry, it's not poisonous. You can trust me," he said with a grin and helped her step closer, his hand steady under her elbow.

The liquid beaded up and ran slowly down the trunk. She pressed her lips to it. Sweet. More came, faster now, like a tap being opened. She drank, careful not to waste any, but stepped back long before she was fully satisfied. Gerald took her place.

She plopped onto the sand, into the shadow of the tree. In a little while, he sat down next to her.

"We can't rest long," he said, scanning the terrain.

"I know." She worried more about him than herself. He was expending a lot of energy by carrying her. Energy he had no way of replacing. If there was one thing she hated, it was not being able to pull her own weight. "You should go on alone. I trust you to come back for me."

"Not a chance."

She had known he would say that. If she were a better person, she might have tried to convince him otherwise. But the truth was, she didn't want to be left behind. She was scared.

They sat together in companionable silence for a few minutes. She wondered what the kids back at the village were doing, how Zaki was managing. They would have stopped by her hut for food by now. Did they worry that she had left them?

"Ready?" Gerald stood then turned, bent his knees and held his hands out.

For a city boy from New York, he sure took to the desert well. After a moment of hesitation, she got on.

He walked at a good pace all through the morning, stopping to rest in the shade of another palm while the worst heat of the day passed. Her ankle was feeling marginally better, but still not good enough to walk on. At least, she could stand unassisted while she drank more palm sap. He wandered around until he found a good handful of green grass stalks, then instructed her how to eat them—to consume the white swollen part just above the root. It had a not unpleasant nutty flavor. He would not take any, but insisted she eat them all. When she had, he told her to get some sleep.

By the time he woke her, the sun was well on its way toward the horizon. They set out without delay. He carried her, same as before, using the time to question her about her work, her background and other projects she was planning for the future. Time seemed to pass faster while her mind was distracted.

They reached the village at nightfall.

ABIGAIL LEANED against the wall and let her eyelids drift closed, glad to be back in her hut, grateful that the mullah's interrogation was over and the man had seemed satisfied with their answers.

"Try to eat a little before you fall asleep."

She opened her eyes and took the strip of smoked lamb Gerald handed her. The faint sounds of wailing filtered in through the door and windows. Abdul's wives were mourning the death of their husband and his sister.

"It's not your fault," Gerald said firmly, reading her mind. "Stop feeling guilty."

"I can't."

He shook his head, but was smiling when he looked at her. "You know, you are not responsible for everything that happens in the universe."

She actually smiled back. "That's what my mother always says."

"Then I guess I can stop now." His grin widened.

He sloshed some water on a piece of rag, brought it over and sat on the floor next to her. "Let me see that ankle."

She pulled up her *abayah* to her knees. He slipped over her heel the elastic that held her narrow-bottom pants in place, lest her ankles showed in public. Her skin was a little discolored, on the purplish side, but not too bad. He ran his finger over the muscles. She held her breath.

He probed gently. "Does this hurt?"

She stared at his large tanned hand moving over her pale skin and, after a few moments when his words finally registered, said, "Not too bad."

He wrapped the wet cloth around her ankle. It sure felt good. Her glance fell on the meat in her hand. She'd forgotten about that. But Gerald was right. The last day or so had taken a lot from both of their bodies. She needed food to build her strength back. She took a bite, listening to the ululating women outside.

Abdul and Leila were gone because of her, no matter what Gerald had said. They would have been nowhere near the bandits if not for her wedding. The mullah had absolved Gerald and her from any responsibility, but she had trouble coming to terms with what had happened. She'd seen the hatred in the dark eyes of Abdul's eldest son. The mullah might not have blamed them, but some of the family did. She swallowed the last of the meal, tasting little of it.

"You'll be fine in a couple of days." Gerald walked away and then came back, bringing another piece of cloth and a pitcher of water. He sat on the dirt floor next to her bed. "Why don't you lie down?"

She did, conscious of every aching muscle. Being carried wouldn't seem like much hardship, but staying in the same position hours on end and hanging on to Gerald had been far from comfortable.

He brushed the hair out of her face and she froze at the intimacy of his touch. Then he pulled away to wet the cloth, used it to gently dab her face, washing off the sweat and sand. All she could do was blink.

His tenderness caught her completely off guard. She'd had him pegged as a lightweight cameraman from the city, but he had shown astounding strength in the desert, and now this new side. She didn't want to like him any more than she already did. Certainly not beyond the superficial level. He would be gone the second that documentary was in the can. One heartbreak per year was her limit.

"There," he said, and they moved at the same time, knocking the pitcher over.

The lukewarm water poured on her shoulder and soaked the mattress.

"Sorry." He dabbed at it and glanced at his sleeping bag. "Why don't you take my place?"

"It'll dry. I wish we had buckets and buckets of water. I'm filthy."

"Tomorrow." He scooped her up and took her to his sleeping bag by the door.

She watched as he ate and drank and lay down on her soggy mattress under the window, stretching his large frame, throwing an arm over his eyes to block the moonlight.

"Thank you," she said.

He didn't respond.

ABIGAIL AWOKE toward dawn, to the sound of Gerald whispering her name.

"What?"

"I heard a noise outside."

She listened, but couldn't detect anything out of the ordinary.

"Stay put." He got up. "I'm going to check it out."

"Probably a stray dog." There were plenty of them in the village.

He shrugged in a way that said "better safe than sorry," then stepped through the door.

She held her breath as she waited, listening for anything unusual. She couldn't hear a thing, not even Gerald's footsteps on the sand. Then a slight sound caught her ear from the direction of the window. She turned her head just in time to see something bright fly in. She heard the sound of glass breaking on the floor, then saw fire. Fire everywhere.

Gerald flew through the door. "Get out! Get out!"

He grabbed her up and ran with her, not stopping until they were at a safe distance. By then, half the hut was ablaze. Heat, worse than the full sun of the desert, sucked the air out of her lungs.

"What was that?" she asked stunned, trembling.

"A firebomb." His breath came in harsh gasps near her ear.

A couple of villagers were running toward them, some with their water jugs. Gerald left her and ran back into the hut, trying to rescue some of their things. He only managed to drag out the sleeping bag by the door when the whole roof caught on fire.

She coughed from the smoke, her eyes watering.

"Get back, dammit. What the hell are you doing?" Gerald dragged her away.

She hadn't realized she had run back to her hut, to him. Everybody was silent, standing back now. They all knew it was too late. The popping and whistling of the fire sounded like some unearthly laughter, and the flames seemed to dance with her meager possessions as if mocking her.

Tears filled her eyes. She was having a really rotten

day. She'd been forced into marriage with a stranger, two people had been killed because of her, she'd been kidnapped by bandits, gotten stranded in the desert, and now her home and everything in it was going up in smoke. She didn't mind her clothes, what little she had, but the thought of precious food burning made her tears spill over. She had children depending on her.

She wiped her eyes, noticing for the first time the throb in her ankle and slid to the ground to take the weight off. She couldn't afford to aggravate the injury, not when she had work to do. She had to rebuild, replenish her supplies.

Gerald squatted next to her. "Are you okay?"

"Who an earth would do something like that?" Then she remembered Abdul's son. He probably blamed them for his father's and aunt's death. "Did you see anyone?"

He shook his head.

"What are we going to do now?"

"I'll find a way to go to Tihrin tomorrow. That's where the foundation is wiring the grant money, to the Banca Internationale. We can get another car and new supplies there. You should let a doctor look at that ankle anyhow."

He sounded so calm, it made her relax a little. Tihrin was twice as big as Rahmara, on the edge of the southern oil fields, a hundred miles or so from Tukatar. It sounded like a very sensible suggestion.

HE HATED doing this to her. Unfortunately, it wasn't his call. If it had been up to him, Abigail wouldn't have gotten involved at all.

In their room at the Hilton in Tihrin, Spike lay on his bed with his hand folded under his head and stared at the ceiling, doing his best to ignore the sound of running water that came from the bathroom. She was taking a shower. Naked.

He was pathetic. He wasn't even attracted to her. He was just puzzled about why she wasn't attracted to him. It seemed strange, and a little annoying. He wished she would come on to him already; then he could gently let her down, and they could both move on. He could stop obsessing about her.

The water stopped, and without thinking, he shifted so he could see her when she came out. She didn't take long. He nearly groaned at the sight of the *abayah* she seemed to wear around the clock. He fought the urge to rip the black cloth off her so he could see just once what was under it. Then he could rest.

At least she didn't have her veil on. Her wet hair was twisted into a bun at her nape, the only way he'd ever seen it. Probably made sense to keep it off her back in this heat. Wet brown strands escaped to frame her face.

He liked redheads and blondes.

"Your turn." Her graceful lips stretched into a smile. She didn't have the kind of swollen, pouty lips he normally went for, and yet he found his glaze glued to them.

"Right." He bounced off the bed. She was distracting him. He couldn't allow that.

He caught the faint fragrance of jasmine as he passed by her and closed the door firmly behind him. The whole bathroom was filled with her scent. Probably the shampoo, one of the few things she'd purchased from the little money she'd been willing to take from him. All she'd bought was one set of new clothes, including *abayah* and veil, and some toiletries. His emergency credit card had been in the pocket of the sleeping bag, the only thing that survived the fire. His wallet was with the bandits. It had been in the Jeep's glove compartment.

The grant money hadn't been wired to the bank yet. The teller checked on its status and promised it would be there first thing in the morning. Until then, Abigail depended on him. He could tell she didn't like it.

He stripped out of his filthy clothes and turned on the water, the cold tap only. He washed the sand out of his hair, his growing beard. It felt good to be clean. He let the cold water wash over him while he planned their day, which was hard to do with a picture of Abigail's lips dancing in his mind.

He shut off the water, grabbed for the fresh clothes he'd bought and dropped the simple long pants and shirt back onto the chair, wrapping the towel around his waist instead. No harm in testing just how resistant Dr. DiMatteo was to him.

He opened the door and leaned against the frame, his arms folded in a way he knew made his biceps bulge.

The rounding of her eyes brought instant gratification. "Where should we go to eat?"

She was lying on top of the covers, her ankle elevated on a pillow. Other women he knew would have stretched luxuriously and given him that come-hither smile he was so familiar with.

She sat up. "Doesn't matter." She looked away from him. "The hotel restaurant is fine."

"I want to take you someplace special." He gave her his absolute best smile. "You won't have to walk. We'll get a cab."

"Okay," she said after a second, with no visible reaction whatsoever.

"You look nice." There. *He* was coming on to *her*.

She didn't look particularly impressed. "I'll call down to the front desk and see if they could recommend a restaurant nearby."

Fine. He stepped back into the bathroom and closed the door behind him.

"WHAT MADE YOU decide to work with war orphans?"

She looked at Gerald over her mutton and rice. He was in documentary-making mode again, which was a tremendous relief, and a great improvement over whatever mode he'd been in up in their hotel room. He'd nearly given her a heart attack when he'd come out of the bathroom practically naked.

She dabbed her lips with the damask napkin. The restaurant was first-rate; Gerald had remembered seeing it somewhere in a tour book. She hadn't wanted anything this fancy, worried about cost, but now, as the food melted on her tongue, she was glad she'd let him talk her into it.

"So originally you're from New Jersey?"

Abigail nodded.

"I was a member of a pro-peace organization at Georgetown University. We put together pamphlets with pictures of starving kids in war-torn countries around the world." It seemed hard to think of starvation next to a table covered with delicacies. "I gave a speech once on the growing threat of land mines, and the research I did for it really opened my eyes. Then when I was in grad school, I had the chance to go to Uganda with the Peace Corps. I ended up doing my Ph.D. on what I learned from that trip."

"I'll have to remember that," he said.

She felt sorry for him. Maybe this assignment was a big deal for his career and here he was without his camera, which had melted in the fire. They would have to spend some time looking around the city for another one before they went back to Tukatar.

"You could be teaching about developing countries at some nice air-conditioned university instead of being kidnapped by bandits in them. How come you didn't stay an academic?"

Good question. It certainly would have been the sensible thing to do. "I almost did. Once you're in the system, it's easy just to progress from one thing to the next. After the Ph.D., I went into teaching. I would have probably gotten tenure eventually. House in the suburbs, the works."

"What's wrong with that?"

A waiter walked by them with a tray of sizzling delicacies, the aroma of honey sauce seducing her senses and distracting her for a moment. The restaurant and the gourmet food it offered were a far cry from Tukatar. It was hard to believe this place was in the same country as her little village. Everything—the furniture, the food, even the table linens—was first-rate. Not a single reminder of the poverty with which most of Beharrain still struggled.

"Dr. DiMatteo, you are a glutton." Gerald was grinning at her.

He was right. She glanced at the plates in front of her. Two were empty and she was working her way through the juicy leg of lamb on the last. When she hadn't been able to decide among three entrées, Gerald had ordered all three for her. She cringed at the terrible excess. Back in Tukatar, she didn't eat this much in a week. But, good Lord, the food was good. She *was* a glutton, no help for it.

"Teaching is wonderful," she said, hoping to turn the attention from her sudden lack of self-control over food. "Nothing wrong with that at all if that's what you want. I just..." She looked at him, wondering if he would understand. Anthony certainly never had. Neither had her parents. "In college I was passionate about issues like war." She looked down at her hands. "Most people know little about what's going on in the world, so they can't do anything about it. Some people are aware, but the situation seems so hopeless. What could one person accomplish? They think it's laughable or incredibly naive even to try. I almost ended up like that."

"But you didn't," he said, holding her gaze. "You're one of the few who's seen reality and given up everything to change it."

"It's not as heroic as that."

"Don't sell yourself short, Abigail."

His approval felt good, even if maybe he just wanted to make her into something bigger than she was because it would look more interesting in his documentary. But maybe he did understand her a little. After all, here he was with her, at the other end of the world. Something had pulled him, as it had pulled her, and, like her, he had answered the call. It seemed insane, but in a sense, she felt closer to him than she had to anyone in a long time. And he was practically a stranger. Well, except for the husband part. That was going to take some getting used to.

A European-looking couple walked by them—German; she recognized the language they spoke. The woman's tongue was just about hanging out as she looked at Gerald.

Abigail rolled her eyes after they passed, then shook her head as Gerald grinned from ear to ear at her reaction. "You know, you're not God's gift to women." The man was cocky beyond belief.

He tugged up his impressive shoulders, looking pretty pleased with himself.

"Don't you want to be liked for more than your muscles and your good looks?"

He went still, his gaze steady on her face, his voice serious when he spoke. "What if there isn't more?"

She narrowed her eyes. Was he fishing for compliments? Of course there was more. He was funny and strong and brave and a million other things she had come to appreciate in the few days they'd spent together.

His self-examination didn't seem to take long. The ever-present grin was back on his face the next minute.

"I think you have an admirer, too. That guy over there keeps looking at you," he said, then added in a voice a notch lower, "He can't have you. You're all mine."

She swallowed, blinked and turned her head in the direction he was looking. The restaurant was filled, only a handful of women among the men. Tihrin was a big city where progress had replaced some old traditions still held rigidly in the countryside. She'd even seen a woman working at the hotel, although she sat in a back room answering phones only, so she wouldn't have to come into face-to-face contact with the male customers.

Abigail scanned the people at each table. Nobody seemed to pay any attention to her. Then a familiar face caught her gaze. "Jamal." He was wearing an olive-green business suit, talking rapidly to the man seated across the table from him.

"Friend of yours?"

"We went to college together. He was friends with my boyfriend at the time." Nate Korsky, the man who had taught her about life outside her own little world, the man who had shown her the way and then refused to follow.

Nate had been a bitter disappointment. A rousing speaker, a passionate peace activist, but it all ended there, with only talk and no action. And then she found out he was arousing more than just high emotions at peace rallies. Apparently he had a number of "close supporters" at a few sororities. Afterward, Anthony, with his maturity, old-world Italian charm and shared culture, had seemed like a knight in shining armor in comparison. He seemed perfect. Her parents adored him, and that deep sexy baritone had seduced her into turning a blind eye to the warning signs that eventually appeared.

"Do you want to go over to say hi before we leave?" Gerald set his fork down and picked up his glass.

They hadn't really known each other that well. Jamal had been more Nate's friend than hers. Still… "Why not?" she said.

But Jamal and his companion rose to leave long before she was done with her meal. She wiped her mouth, watching as they made their way among the tables toward her. Luckily, Gerald had picked a table right by the door so the men had to walk by them to get out.

"Jamal?"

He stopped and looked at her.

"Abigail DiMatteo. Remember? Nate Korsky's girlfriend from Georgetown."

His aristocratic mouth immediately stretched into a warm smile. "Abigail? Forgive me, I didn't recognize you dressed like this," he said in nearly unaccented English.

Gerald stood and extended his hand. "Hi, I'm Gerald Thornton, Abigail's husband. Would you join us for coffee?"

Jamal hesitated for a moment. "Certainly. Excuse me for a second."

He walked his companion to the door, where they talked for another minute or two, and then he returned to their table.

"What are you doing here?" he asked Abigail.

"I work in Tukatar, starting up a program for war orphans."

"Still trying to save the world?" He flashed her a warm smile then turned to Gerald. "And you?"

"I'm filming her work to prepare a documentary. Well, I was filming." He shrugged. "Our hut was firebombed yesterday, so for the moment we are without a home or supplies."

She knew what was coming before Jamal even opened his mouth and could have kicked Gerald under the table for it.

"You must stay at my home. I would love to have you as my guests for as long as you would like."

Middle Eastern hospitality allowed no other answer.

"That's very kind of you, but we got a room at the Hilton. We'll be fine."

"I insist. I could not let my friends stay at a hotel when my home is so close to the city. May I send a car for you later?"

"That would be lovely. Thank you," she said, knowing that to refuse would have been incredibly rude, if not an outright offense.

Chapter Four

Spike looked around the room and wished Jamal had sent Abigail to the women's quarters. Rooming together would make it harder to place the dozen or so bugs he had hidden in the secret compartment of his sandal before burning down the hut.

He would distribute the bugs then get Abigail out of there as fast as he could. Once he told the Colonel his mission had been accomplished, a surveillance team would be sent in with the proper equipment. They could pick up whatever was said in the house without having to come within a hundred feet. And hopefully, what they heard would lead them to Suhaib. Fast.

His role in the operation was a relatively minor one, unfortunately, close to being completed. He'd been put on the job as a precaution, in case anything untoward had to be done—such as blackmailing or forcing Dr. DiMatteo if she were uncooperative. Or if successful completion of the mission called for something grossly illegal. As a member of the SDDU, a secret military unit whose existence was known only by a select few, he could get away with a hell of a lot. More than members of any government agency or military branch that actually had to report their activities to a string of superiors and were closely watched by Congress.

But everything had gone smoothly so far. The fact that he hadn't been able to recruit and train Abigail was a minor glitch. It would have been better if she had been able to conduct the mission on her own. A lot less suspicious. The original plan didn't call for him at this stage, only as distant support. Still, now that he was in, he was glad for it. There were too many unknowns in a house of this size to properly train a novice for every possibility. He would place the bugs; then they'd get out before anyone caught on and had a chance to dig into Gerald Thornton's background.

Once Abigail was safely back in Tukatar, he would see if the Colonel would let him in on the action at the takedown. Having come this far, he didn't want to miss out on all the excitement.

Hearing footsteps outside the door, he stepped to the side, instantly alert. He could not afford to let his guard down as long as they were in this house. The sound of heels on stone came closer, then stopped. A woman. Still, he would not allow himself to relax.

The door opened and so did his mouth, but no sound came out. Abigail?

The *abayah* was gone. She wore a pale green figure-hugging pantsuit. *Yes, sir!* The sight of her made his throat go dry. Her bun was down, her auburn locks swaying around her face, falling to the middle of her back.

She twirled around laughing, as excited as a teenager at a mall shopping spree. "Chanel. I got set up by one of Jamal's sisters. You wouldn't believe what these women wear under their *abayah*s."

"Wow." His brain kicked into gear finally, and he was suddenly aware of the room for more than its strategic qualities such as where they could take cover in the event of gunfire. For the first time, he registered the silk sheets and velvet pillows, the sheer curtains that flanked not only the narrow windows high up the wall but also the antique four-poster bed with its extensive gilded carvings. The room was meant for seduction. And here in front of him was Scheherazade.

She came closer.

He offered her a nonchalant smile. "Want to rest before dinner?" Any excuse to get her to the bed.

Her eyes, the rich brown color of the smoothest Belgian chocolate, widened. It seemed ridiculous that he'd ever thought her less than gorgeous. She had the kind of natural, wholesome beauty he had not understood enough before to appreciate. Now he wondered why he'd ever thought the artifice of makeup and a fancy hairstyle could hope to compete with that. Her gaze was filled with such longing, it seared through him.

He lowered his voice. "What are you thinking about?"

"That I would give anything for a big bowl of spaghetti and meatballs with gravy," she said. "Not that I don't like the local delicacies, it's just…it would be nice to have something familiar every once in a while."

He appreciated the irony of the situation. They were alone in a bedroom straight from a dream, and all she wanted was a bowl of spaghetti. Disappointment slapped him back into rational thinking. "I know what you mean. I'm dying for a cold Budweiser." Among other things.

She laughed again, and the soft sound skittered across his skin. She was set on driving him crazy. He couldn't be distracted now. He was here to do a job. He had to get her out of his blood.

"Abby?" He took another step toward her.

"Mmm?" She was looking at the fruit basket on the octagonal handpainted table by the door.

"Are you attracted to me at all?"

Her gaze snapped back to him. "Not really," she said without breathing.

She was lying like a rug. He could tell from the way she fidgeted.

It was simple. He had a mission and she was distracting him from it. He had no choice but to neutralize his attraction. She was like a glass of ice water dangled in front of a thirsty man. All he had to do was to take a sip and be done with it, release himself from her strange hold and move on to what he was here to do.

"You owe me a wedding kiss," he said in his best seductive voice.

She was staring at him, alarmed. "It was a pretend wedding."

"A pretend kiss, then." He moved closer and lowered his head, brushing his lips against hers. And embarrassed himself by groaning. Her lips were as soft as silk. One touch was not enough. Just a little more and he could say, "Been there, done that" and walk away.

He nibbled on her lower lip playfully, holding back the urgency that rushed through his veins. When he licked the seam of her lips, she parted them in surprise. He wouldn't have been a good soldier if he didn't press forward when given an advantage.

She tasted like mint. His hands sought her, brought her closer; his fingers were lost in her lustrous hair, getting tangled just as he was getting tangled in the force of unexpected sensations. He was going too far. He had to stop.

But it was she who pulled away. "That was pretend?" Her voice sounded weak.

He took a deep breath. "Absolutely." He was pretending like hell that she hadn't just rocked his world.

She searched his face. "Gerald, I—"

"Call me Spike," he said, and kissed her again.

He'd made a mistake thinking one kiss would be enough. Her body fitted his perfectly, and there was no hiding how much he wanted her. And yet, this was neither the time nor the place. Even if it was, Abigail was not the right type of woman. Maybe he could seduce her—God knew, he wanted to—but she deserved more.

And what if he did seduce her and found even that was not enough?

"Mr. Hareb would like to request the pleasure of your company at dinner, if you would join him at your earliest convenience." A disembodied voice spoke from the room's intercom.

Spike pulled away, his head reeling. "We better go."

"Yeah," she said, slightly dazed, her eyes swirling with confusion, her lips swollen with his kiss.

He walked to the door and opened it for her, knowing it was best that they got out of there right now.

They walked down the opulent hallway—enemy territory, he reminded himself, on alert again. He forced his mind to the task and counted the doors on each side, hoping to get some sense of the layout of the house. The front door where they had come in was farther from their room than he would have liked. Maybe there was a nearer point of exit. Finding that out was one of the first things on his list—just in case. But he didn't get the chance to nose around much. A servant waited at the end of the hall to escort them to dinner.

They followed him to a large room where about a dozen people sat around a western-style dining room set. Their host had money *and* good taste, a rare combination. Spike's glance slid from one oil painting on the wall to another.

"Ahlan wa sahlan." Jamal welcomed them as he rose to introduce his family: his mother, his wife, two brothers and their wives, who were visiting. The women

looked slightly uncomfortable, some of the men suspicious. Clearly, Jamal's family was not as accustomed to western ways as he was.

"*Shukran.*" Spike thanked him for his hospitality and exchanged the customary pleasantries, while trying to take the measure of the man. Just how involved was he in his youngest brother's activities? How westernized had he become while attending university in the U.S.? Could he be, given sufficient incentive, turned against his brother?

Spike sat and crossed his legs, his right calf on his left knee. He rested his left hand on his ankle, his sandal and the dozen or so bugs in the secret compartment within easy reach. He retrieved one and pressed it on the underside of the table while reaching for his glass with his other hand.

ABIGAIL CLOSED the door behind her. Gerald wasn't back yet. Good. He'd been invited to join the men after dinner to enjoy the water pipe. She hoped he'd stay a while. She needed a little distance from the man.

Spike? She grinned and shook her head at the nickname. There had to be a story behind that. The man was full of surprises.

The kiss for one. What on earth was that about? And she couldn't really blame him. It wasn't as if she'd been screaming no. On the contrary, she'd nearly melted on the spot. So they had chemistry. Now what? Ignoring it seemed like the best thing to do. He would make his documentary and be gone, hopefully soon. Then she could return to her ordinary life—after the few years it would take to forget him.

Once she had the foundation's money and made a few improvements in the village, if all went well the mullah would be impressed enough to let her stay, even without a husband in residence. A man traveling for work and leaving his wife behind for extended periods of time wasn't all that unusual.

She walked to the bed to drop her armload of clothes on the sumptuous coverlet, touched by the women's extreme generosity. They had neither seen nor heard of her before today, and yet they treated her as a longtime friend. She'd been taken by Jamal's wife and sisters-in-law back to his sisters' rooms. The two girls—one seventeen, the other nineteen—had not been present at dinner, not allowed in the presence of a strange man, as they were unmarried.

She sat next to the pile and looked at the white phone on the carved bedside table. She'd been invited to make as many calls as she liked. She picked up the receiver and dialed her parents' number. Since she'd last talked to her mother—fought with her, more specifically—she'd been nearly killed twice. Once by the bandits and once by the fire. She would never actually tell Mom that, or she would never hear the end of the nagging, but she felt the need to touch base. To make things better between them than the last time they left it.

The phone rang five times before the answering machine picked up. "It's me," she said. "Just thought I'd check in. Everything is okay here. Miss you." She took a deep breath. "I love you both."

The door behind her opened and closed. She set down the receiver and turned around.

"Anything exciting?" Gerald asked with one of those disarming smiles that always stole her breath.

"Not here."

He threw her a questioning look, amusement glinting in the corner of his eyes. "About—before we went to dinner—"

"Would you like to use the phone?" She shot up from the bed and gathered the clothes in her arms. She should hang them up before they got wrinkled. "We could buy a new battery for your cell phone while we're out shopping together. Or you could ask Jamal if he has a charger that would work. You probably have people to check in with."

He shook his head. "No family. No significant other."

Great. She had meant to imply someone like his boss at the foundation, and not come off sounding as if she were fishing to find out whether he had a girlfriend at home. But now that he had volunteered the information… His quick "no significant other" was awfully hard to believe. She had no doubt whatsoever that women threw themselves at him wherever he went.

He kicked off his sandals and stretched. "Ready for bed?"

She dropped the clothes back on the coverlet. Not on purpose. Her muscles just let go. The sight of him, combined with those words, was mind-boggling. Especially in light of what they were doing before dinner. "I think I'll check in with the university."

"Mind if I take the bathroom first, then?"

"Go ahead." She reached for the phone, welcoming the excuse to turn from him.

She couldn't handle Gerald Thornton, and that was the truth. He was way out of her league. He had heartache written all over him. And now that their relationship had crossed from professional to—well, wherever it had crossed to—she wasn't ready for it. Okay, she was more than ready for it, but she was also smart enough to know better than to act on her impractical impulses.

TWO AMERICANS in the house. El Jafar drew on the water pipe, considering every possibility one by one. He didn't believe in coincidences.

He had to get rid of them one way or the other. Now was definitely not the time to entertain strangers.

First, he had to figure out whether they had a secret agenda or were speaking the truth. Most westerners in his country were liars and thieves. But the two Americans' sudden disappearance would draw attention. He could only risk that if he was sure the deed had to be done.

If indeed, they were in Tihrin as a result of a series

of misfortunes, he would donate money to their cause and send them on their way. Fast. He had no time to waste.

But first, he had to determine which way to deal with them. He glanced at the handful of computer printouts Ahmad brought over. His cousin was good at anything that had to do with computers, especially when it came to the bottomless resources of the Internet.

Dr. Abigail DiMatteo. El Jafar looked at the grainy picture from her home page on the university's Web site. Her background with the Peace Corps and everything else she'd said about herself checked out.

He shuffled the papers and spread out the sheets that confirmed Gerald Thornton's claims—reviews of documentaries that mentioned his name. No picture of him. El Jafar tossed the printouts aside and stood. The information Ahmad had found should have set him at ease. It didn't.

Neither of the guests had acted suspiciously. He could swear every word the woman had spoken was the truth. The man, Thornton, was harder to read, but seemingly open and relaxed. And yet, their presence in the house prickled his instincts.

He sat and reached for the pipe again. If the foreigners were up to something, he would know it soon. He had made sure they were most closely watched.

SPIKE LAY on top of the covers, his eyes fixed on the bathroom door. It shouldn't take her too long to clean up. They'd both taken showers earlier, as soon as they'd been shown to their room. He wore nothing but his black boxer shorts, wanting to make her as uncomfortable as possible so she would turn in to sleep right away. He needed the night to search the house and place his bugs.

And yet, when the door opened and she came out, he wasn't prepared for it. Nightgowns like that should come with a warning label from the American Heart Association. The bathroom light behind her outlined her figure through the sheer material, hiding little. Then she reached back and flipped the switch off.

Damn. "You're too thin," he said gruffly and tried to focus on that, rather than on the number of other highly inappropriate ideas that swarmed in his head.

"We're in the middle of a famine." She walked to the light switch by the door and turned that off, too. It didn't make much of a difference; enough moonlight came through the windows to illuminate the room.

"Are you eating enough?" It seemed safer to focus on that topic than on the fact that she would be in bed with him in the matter of seconds. Technically, it was their honeymoon.

"Stop acting like my mother." She climbed under the covers and settled in as far away from him as the spacious bed allowed.

"Sorry. Good night, Abigail."

"Good night, Gerald."

"My friends call me Spike."

She turned toward him. "I've been wondering. Where did that come from?"

He was reluctant to tell her anything personal—the less she knew, the better. But since he'd been stupid enough to tell her to call him Spike, he had to give some kind of explanation. "I was in an accident a long time ago. Got my skull busted so they had to put these screws in. They stuck out on top like a Mohawk." He'd gotten frisky with a bomb during his SDDU training—on a dare. It had nearly gotten him kicked out of the group.

"Good night, Spike," she said and closed her eyes.

She was not dazzling in the traditional sense of the word, but had this inner peace, a certain strength, that reflected in her face and made her hard to ignore. Her arm, slimmer than it should have been, lay gracefully on the top of the covers. He would bet anything that she'd been giving up half her meals to the kids since she'd been in Beharrain.

She faked sleep for the longest time, but then her breathing finally evened. He waited another twenty minutes to make sure she was fully, deeply asleep before he slipped from the bed, pulled on his clothes and then sneaked out the door without making a sound.

He hesitated for a moment. He didn't like leaving her unprotected. Didn't like leaving her, period. But the sooner he accomplished his mission, the sooner he could get her out of there and away from any possible danger. He crept forward.

The hallway was empty. No security cameras. He had picked up on that earlier. The perimeter and the entrance had cameras and a massive security system, but once in the house, he hadn't seen any. He heard voices in the distance—men talking, too far to make out the words. They didn't seem to be coming closer. He took a minute to search for hidden cameras and found a dozen likely spots among the ornately carved wall decorations, but nothing on closer observation. He moved on.

He would search the main house tonight, then the outbuildings tomorrow night—Jamal had invited them to stay as long as they liked. Outside would be trickier. He would have to avoid the guards, the security cameras and the dogs.

He walked down the hallway to the end where it came to a tee. They had gone to the left for dinner earlier. He looked right and was pretty sure that way led to the bedrooms, so he went left, hoping to find Jamal's office.

He heard footsteps ahead. Somebody was coming his way. He backed into the dining room and waited until whoever was out in the hallway had passed. Then he opened the door a crack and watched the servant's back until he disappeared from sight. Maybe he should follow the man. He considered that for a moment but decided against it. He wanted to get a better sense of the house's layout first. Right now, he could easily become trapped.

He crept to the next door down the hall and listened for a while before testing the doorknob. It opened silently into a small storage room of some sort. He moved on.

Another half hour passed before he found what he was looking for—a locked door. Bingo. He took off his watch and extracted the slim metal pick from the back. The lock gave in seconds. He stepped in and closed the door behind him, listening in the dark, windowless room. Not a sound in there other than his own breathing.

All was quiet in the hall, too. He flipped on the light just long enough to get the lay of the room, then turned it off again. With care, he made his way over to one of the two desks in the large state-of-the-art-equipped room and turned on the computer. Password-protected.

He'd expected as much. It would delay him, but could not stop him. He would call the Colonel as soon as they were out in the city tomorrow. He had every confidence the man could get the proper software to him within twenty-four hours. Tonight's job was more of a reconnaissance mission.

He left the screen on and used its light to riffle through the papers on the desk. Bills, invoices, business correspondence. Nothing suspicious. He picked the lock on the drawers, but didn't come up with anything usable there, either. Maybe the other desk. He walked over and turned the laptop on, more for the light its screen would provide than because he thought he would be able to access it. He merely nodded when the password protection window came on.

He went through the drawers and the small filing cabinet. More business documents, maps, a handgun—9 mm Smith & Wesson—shoved far in the back. Loaded. He hesitated for a moment, wanting to take it, hating that he'd been without his SIG since he had entered the country—part of his cover. But if he took the gun, chances were it would be missed. He couldn't risk discovery. For now it would have to be enough that he knew where it was.

He searched through the bookcases, looking for hidden compartments, and came up empty. He made sure he locked every drawer and cabinet the way he had found it, then turned off the screens. When he heard no sound out in the hallway, he opened the door inch by inch. All clear. He stepped outside and locked the door behind him.

He glanced at his watch. Just after midnight. Plenty of time to look around some more. He had seen the outside entry to the cellar when they got out of the car Jamal had sent for them. He hoped there was a way to get down there from the inside, as well. He moved forward as silently as a shadow, determined to find it.

He stumbled onto it an hour later in the kitchen. The jars of honey on the top of the trapdoor indicated that it wasn't used regularly. He moved everything aside, neatly tucked next to the wall, so it wouldn't be immediately obvious that they were out of place if somebody happened to walk into the kitchen for a midnight snack.

He swiped a box of matches from one of the tables,

lifted the wood panel and then descended into the darkness one careful step after the other. Once he closed the door behind him, he lit a match.

Crates of guns, ammunition and hand grenades towered to the ceiling. The CIA had been right. El Jafar did keep in touch with his family. More than in touch. From the looks of it, they were helping him. It would be only a matter of time before the bugs would pick up something. Hopefully sooner than later. He would stick a few bugs in the cellar, then call it quits for the night—do the rest tomorrow. He wanted to be back in the room before Abigail woke up and came looking for him.

The match burned to the tip of his fingers; he pinched the flame out and lit another. He put a bug inside one of the crates and another under a low table by the wall. A muffled noise came from above. He put out the match. Somebody was in the kitchen.

Voices sounded from outside, too. He stepped behind a stack of crates just in time before the cellar door opened and light flooded the room.

"You've been a busy man, Mr. Thornton." Jamal's voice rang out.

Spike kept his cover and moved toward the open crate of rifles in the back, hoping he would have the time to load one.

"Maybe if you told me what you were looking for, I could help you find it?" Jamal continued. "Come on out now. No sense of hiding. You've tripped every silent alarm in your wake. I was just waiting until you got somewhere I could trap you without waking the whole house."

Jamal was definitely in with his brother. Deeper than they had thought. He was a successful, American-educated businessman, the most progressive person in his family, pro-reform. As the oldest son and the family's patriarch since their father's death, he had been questioned about his brother's whereabouts, had claimed Suhaib had been kicked out of the family by their father years ago and had been out of contact since then.

The CIA had been skeptical about that. In this part of the world, family ties were everything. But although they had suspected tacit support, they didn't think Jamal was in on the action. Their investigation had failed to turn that up. His involvement sure as hell raised the stakes. And put Abigail in danger.

Spike grabbed a rifle without making a sound, and looked through a small gap in between crates. Jamal had about a dozen men with him, all armed to the teeth. He hoped none of them was stupid enough to start shooting in there.

But, of course, despite Jamal's hand in the air holding them back, one of them did. And once the first shot rang out, there was no stopping the rest. He loaded the rifle and lunged for the trapdoor to the kitchen. Blocked. Whoever was up there wasn't letting him out.

Then the crates exploded, and the house shook—the ceiling, the walls, even the dirt floor beneath him. The splitting pain in his head was the last thing he felt.

Chapter Five

She was in her hut, trapped by flames, screaming for Spike. And then the walls exploded. Abigail sat up in the bed, disoriented. A bad dream—no. She looked at the phone that had been knocked onto the floor, her ears ringing. The explosion had been real.

She was alone in bed.

"Spike?"

The bathroom door stood open. He wasn't in there.

She threw the *abayah* over her nightgown, the veil on her head, and rushed to the door, pulled it open. The two armed guards outside outyelled each other, their guns immediately trained on her.

"What happened?" she asked in her best Arabic.

They ignored her question. One of them used the long barrel of his gun to shove her back. Another man rushed down the hall, his clothes covered in plaster, his face bleeding. Jamal. He was yelling instructions she didn't understand.

"Are you all right? What's going on?"

He didn't even look at her as he hurried by.

The two men pushed her into the room and came in after her. One of them swung his rifle onto his back, while the other kept his pointed straight at her head. She got the idea. If she resisted, she was toast.

Her arms and legs were tied before she knew what was going on, her questions halted when the man knocked her down, knelt on her chest and gagged her. They rolled her up unceremoniously in the Persian carpet she'd admired earlier; then she was being lifted. A punch into her stomach knocked the air out of her. No, it wasn't a punch. One of them had thrown her over his shoulder, she realized as they began moving. She was rolled up tight, the dirty cloth stuffed into her mouth, gagging her. With each breath she sucked in the dusty-smelling air from the carpet.

She refused to let panic engulf her. She had to figure out what was going on, she had to come up with a plan. She was being kidnapped for some reason. By an old friend from college. Not that good a friend, obviously.

She could almost hear her mother's voice in her head. *Be sensible, Abigail. You can't possibly mean to go over there. You'll be kidnapped and sold into white slavery or into some harem as a sex slave. These things happen, you know.*

She doubted very much that Jamal Hareb was dealing in sex slaves. But then what an earth did he plan to do with her? Her instincts said she wasn't headed for a plush little harem.

She heard voices as more men joined the ones who were taking her God knew where. Dogs barked. They were outside. She heard a motor start and another; she could smell the exhaust. Then she was dropped, smashing her shoulder against something hard. The ground vibrated under her. No, not the ground. She was in the back of a truck. And not alone. A couple of men were talking above her, bracing her with their feet so she wouldn't roll as the vehicle began to move.

She tried to ignore the pain and concentrate on what they were saying. Not much, probably aware that she could hear and understand them. Two of them had been injured in the explosion, the talk focused on that.

The explosion, Spike missing and her being kidnapped—they were all connected somehow. The truck stopped, but only for a minute before taking off again. Probably a traffic light. Where were they going? And what would they do to her when they got there?

Maybe her mother had been right. She should have stayed home and married Anthony. She would have been unhappy, but at least alive. Life was full of tradeoffs.

She lost track of time, rattling in the back of the truck as it picked up speed. They must have left the city behind finally. Her limbs had gone numb from lack of movement, her shoulder pulsed with pain. The longer she lay there, the grimmer her thoughts turned. Maybe they were taking her out into the desert to shoot and bury her.

She had to find a way to get away from them. Knowing what was going on would have helped.

Spike had sneaked out of their room in the middle of the night. If he'd been taken by force, she would have woken up. He was a big man; she couldn't imagine him being taken without a heck of a struggle. No, he had left on his own. But why?

Had he caused the explosion?

It made no sense. Jamal had offered them his hospitality. Spike had seemed eager to accept it, pleased to be allowed inside such a prominent family's home. The more he learned about the country, the better his documentary would be. If he was a cameraman… The doubts she'd had about him after the attack of the bandits now returned with a rush.

Only two possibilities existed—either he'd caused the explosion or he hadn't. If he hadn't, then who had? Presumably no one in Jamal's family would want to blow up his own house. A business rival? But then why was she rolled up in a carpet?

And if Spike had caused the explosion? This theory made more sense than the first. If he had blown up something, Jamal might have thought she was in on it. But the question remained: Why would Spike do this? If he wasn't Gerald Thornton, the Barnsley Foundation's cameraman, then who was he?

She had forgotten her doubts about him in the scare of the firebomb and all that had followed. What if the firebomb hadn't been from one of the villagers who resented her being there? What if it hadn't been from Abdul's son? What if it had been meant for Spike? But from whom?

She supposed a secret agent would have some enemies. And she was becoming more and more convinced that was what he was. Some kind of a government operative. Her first instinct had been right. And it really, really ticked her off that he would use her as a pawn in some insane plot, risking her life and undermining her work. If he hadn't died in the explosion, he was going to wish he had once she was through with him.

After an eternity, the truck stopped, and she was lifted up by two men, one on each end. They carried her somewhere. She could hear doors open and close. Then she was put down, with care this time instead of being dropped, and she was grateful for the small mercy for a second before someone gave her a good kick to unroll her from the carpet.

The light bulb hanging from a wire above blinded her. A door banged shut. She squeezed her eyelids together then opened them again after a little while. She was alone in a small prison cell-like room, still bound and gagged. And she was pretty sure she wasn't going to leave there alive.

She lifted her hands and removed the cloth jammed into her mouth. Marginally better. But she didn't have time to enjoy the relatively small comfort before a man dressed in a camouflage uniform came for her and loosened the ropes around her ankles enough so she could walk, then dragged her from the room.

"Where are you taking me?" she asked in Arabic.

He spit in her face. The tobacco-smelling slime ran down her skin, into the neck of the *abayah*. The man held her by one arm so she couldn't even lift her hand to her cheek. She tried to wipe her face on her shoulder instead, grateful when she partially succeeded.

They went down a narrow hallway and turned left. Then he shoved her into a larger sparsely furnished room. A young man resembling Jamal, dressed in a camouflage uniform, sat on a couple of sandbags. He couldn't have been more than twenty-five. A chair stood in the corner, a table next to it with a funky radio. The smell of garlic hung in the air. The guard who had brought her in took her to the chair and shoved her down hard.

"I don't understand—"

"How long have you known Gerald Thornton?" the young man, obviously in charge, questioned her.

"A couple of days."

She bit back a moan as ropes cut into her flesh. She was being tied to the chair.

"But he's your husband now. Why the sudden marriage? It is hardly your custom."

This was no time to lie. She told him about the mullah, and how they had gotten married so they could stay and work in Tukatar.

"So you make fun of our customs and religion by this mock marriage." The muscles in his cheeks tightened.

"Not at all." She fought the desperation that came from knowing whatever she would say he would turn against her. "We were trying to obey your laws."

"What do you know about him?"

Not a lot. She focused on the table and the radio in front of her. And realized it wasn't a radio. She swallowed.

"He works for the Barnsley Foundation. He's a cameraman. He doesn't have a family. He's a good driver. Speaks excellent Arabic." Until now, she hadn't realized how every time they had talked, Spike had always managed to turn the conversation to her. It hadn't seemed strange or suspicious at the time. He was there, after all, to make a documentary about her work.

"Anything else?"

She shook her head.

The man nodded to the guard. He picked up the electrodes from the table, lifted them to her forehead. She thrashed wildly, jerking her head from side to side, until the young man got up and came over to hold her down. His hands on either side of her face, he forced her to stay still until the electrodes were stuck to her forehead. He stepped away.

She hadn't known before such panic existed. She was awash in it, petrified. Had she had any information, she would have given it to them. "Please, no. I don't know anything. I'm here to help the children—"

The first jolt of electricity shot through her and she convulsed hard, biting her tongue, tasting blood.

Then the pain stopped as suddenly as it began. Her panic did not. But she was still alive. She tried to focus on that as she gasped for air, frantic to come up with something that would stop the torture.

"What do you know about Gerald Thornton?" The young man now stood in front of her, his face hard-set. There'd be no mercy coming from him.

Tears sprung to her eyes. "Nothing—"

He nodded to the guard and the pain began again.

SPIKE CAME AROUND, his ears ringing, every bone in his body feeling broken. His arms and legs were tied together. Damn. He opened his eyes slowly. He was in a small cell. Not alone. But the guard with him left as soon as he saw his eyes open. The key turned in the lock.

He prepared himself for the coming pain, knowing he didn't have long. He was right. No more than five minutes passed before the door opened and Jamal's youngest brother came in with three of his men. Suhaib Hareb. El Jafar. He looked thinner and grimmer than the picture in his CIA file.

"Where is Abigail?"

"It's amazing how little your wife knows about you, Mr. Thornton," he said in Arabic.

"What have you done to her?"

"She insisted she didn't know why you were here." He paused. "My brother seems to think she might be telling the truth. I'm inclined to agree."

Then they no longer needed her—in which case, she was probably already dead. The thought hit him harder than he would have expected, a tightness in his gut that squeezed till he hurt. Damn.

This was exactly what was wrong with bringing civilians into an operation. They had all known something like this could happen—the CIA, the Colonel, him. And they had gone ahead with the plan anyhow. Bitter regret rose in his chest. He was more than comfortable fighting any enemy, but civilian casualties got to him. And Abigail—he closed his eyes for a moment. He should have never dragged her into this.

Suhaib came closer. "You tell me what I want to know, and I'll let her go."

He had expected a bargain like that. It didn't mean she was still alive. "I want to see her first." He stalled for time.

"You're hardly in position to make demands. I don't think you fully appreciate your predicament."

"The police are probably investigating the explosion already. They'll look for us. They know at the Hilton where we went."

Suhaib shrugged. "They'll be told the servants' kids found a land mine in the fields and brought it home. Boys are always curious about things like that. Very unfortunate, but it's happened before. The police will be told that the Americans got spooked and decided to leave."

"You're not going to get away with this as easily."

Suhaib looked at him for a long moment. "Maybe not forever, but long enough," he said, then turned and left, his hands folded behind his back.

His men remained.

Spike strained against his binds. They had tied him tight. It would take time to loosen the ropes, if he could do it at all. And he had no time, or rather, just enough to curl up to protect his head before the first boot connected with an already broken rib.

Son of a bitch. That hurt. He jackknifed his body, kicking the feet out from under one of the men. The guy hit his head against the stone wall in a tremendous stroke of luck and went limp on the floor. The other two pummeled Spike with double savagery.

He ignored the pain, twisted and grabbed for the boot that was coming toward him, twisted again and pulled the man down. Within seconds, his attacker's head was between Gerald's knees as he tried to crush the man's windpipe.

But then the butt of the third man's rifle came down on his temple and that was the end of that.

THEY WERE dragging her somewhere again. Didn't matter. It would be over soon. She couldn't take much more, and they knew it. Abigail squinted against the bright sun as an outside door opened in front of her.

She couldn't walk so they dragged her along by her arms, her feet dangling in the hot sand. She couldn't remember when she had lost the beautiful hand-embroidered slippers one of Jamal's sisters had given her. The opulent mansion and the kindness of the women seemed as if they had been in another lifetime.

Half a dozen buildings stood in haphazard order around them, part of some kind of training course visible behind one. The sun beat mercilessly through the giant camouflage netting that stretched above the buildings. She'd seen enough footage of terrorist camps on TV to recognize this as one.

The men dragged her to a small trailer in the middle and down a short hallway. One of them unlocked a door and opened it; the other shoved her into the darkness. She fell forward, hitting her knees and elbows. The pain brought tears to her eyes. The door slammed shut behind her.

She was alone. No. The short hairs on her nape stood up at the sound of shallow breathing. Somebody or something was in there with her. She scampered away from the sound until her back touched the wall. Maybe they were going to feed her to some kind of beast. She fought the panic, listening for any sound of movement, struggling to stand.

Something growled. A scream rose in her throat, but then the sound came again, and she realized it wasn't a growl after all, but a groan. Decidedly human.

"Spike?"

No response.

"Spike?" *Please, please, please, God. Let it be him.*

"Over here." His voice was raspy, weak.

She hobbled forward and promptly fell over him. He groaned again.

"Sorry." She rolled off. "Are you okay?"

"I wasn't—" He took a deep shuddering breath. "I wasn't sure you were still here."

"I don't think they're going to let either of us go."

"Are you hurt?"

"I'm fine. Alive." But for how long? "What's going on?"

Silence stretched between them, and she suddenly remembered he was the reason they were here. She'd forgotten all about that in her relief that it was him in the cell with her instead of a ravenous beast.

"I hate you," she said at last. Every word he had ever said to her had been a lie. God, she'd been stupid beyond belief. How had she not figured this out before? "You had no right."

"I know." His somber voice reached her in the darkness. "The only reason they put us together is if they're somehow listening."

Right. She understood what he meant. He couldn't tell her anything. So he really was a secret agent or something like that. Her anger grew. How dare he gamble with her life? She had never hit anyone, but the urge to find him in the dark and pummel him seemed irresistible. And yet, as strong as her anger was, her will to live was stronger. She took a couple of deep breaths. She could yell at him later. Right now, they had to stick together. They had to find a way to escape.

"We haven't done anything and we don't know anything. We're only in Beharrain to help the kids," she said.

"Right."

She could hear the relief in his voice. And something else. Exhaustion? Pain? "Are you hurt?"

He crawled next to her, his breath hot on her wrist. "I'm pretty much done in. I don't think I have a single rib unbroken."

She wondered how much of that was true, and how much was what he wanted them to hear. She felt something tug at her ropes, and understood what he was trying to do—loosen her bonds with his teeth.

"I'm okay now," she said. "Just sore and exhausted. No matter what they do to me, I can't tell them anything more than I already have." She kept on talking, carrying on her one-sided conversation, covering up for the fact that he was using his mouth for something else.

"I hope they'll let us go soon. My mother has a tendency to go nuts if I don't check in every couple of days. She'll be calling every senator in Washington demanding they send in the army. She lost a child already, so she's a little on the paranoid side when it comes to me. I'm the only one left." She turned her hands to make his work easier.

The ropes didn't give, however, and he gave up after a while.

"I'm sure your sister's death was hard on all of you. Leukemia is a terrible disease."

Right. He would know all that. Her entire private life was probably neatly typed up, sitting in some file somewhere. He probably knew everything there was to know about her. How dare they?

"I'm sorry," he said.

She was too mad to respond. They sat in silence for some time.

"Do you think they'll kill us?" she blurted out the question that filled her mind.

"I doubt it. If we disappeared, the U.S. would investigate. Dozens of people saw us with Jamal Hareb at the restaurant. The people at the hotel know that's where we went. Investigators would be at his door in no time. I'm sure he wishes to bring no shame to his family."

She could hear him move around, then felt his fingers on her hand. He was tugging on her ropes again.

"What do you think will happen?"

"My bet is that he'll keep us around so he can use us at the right time for bargaining."

Sounded good, except that the U.S. didn't negotiate with terrorists. But of course, Spike's words weren't meant for her reassurance. They were meant to convince whoever was listening that the two Americans were worth keeping alive, keeping around. And that might give Spike and her a chance to escape. She really hoped he had a plan.

"What are you going to do once your project in Tukatar is up and running?"

She doubted he cared. Most likely he wanted whoever was listening to know her work in the country was real and not connected to bringing down terrorist organizations. Better to talk about her project than think about the many ways they could torture her to death.

"Transition it to the locals, then move on to the next town." Getting the kids off the streets would be a big improvement. She wanted them to have shelter and food. The government had no money to build and maintain orphanages, that was for sure. She had to help the children to help themselves. "Who knows, with a working example or two, the project might gain some attention."

"The media love a success story."

"Exactly. More international aid would be wonderful." Of course, that kind of stuff was always very undependable. Attention invariably fell on other new areas and the money was often redirected there without warning. "Foreign aid is valuable, but to make things work in the long run, you need a plan that'll work without it."

"Self-sustaining communities," he quoted one of the headlines from her grant proposal.

"Right. That's why I'm encouraging the children to learn marketable skills." They needed those to survive right now in the postwar economy. "I also hope to give them some rudimentary education that will help them in the future." She fell silent.

"Trying to save the world, huh?"

"No one person can save the world. But I know a couple of kids in Tukatar—"

"How did you pick that place?"

"It's a long story."

"Looks like we have time."

But in the end, they didn't. Not a minute passed before the door slammed open to admit two men who grabbed her. She barely had the chance to glance back before they dragged her out. The light coming through the door fell on Spike. She gasped at the sight. His face was beaten nearly beyond recognition. It looked like his cheekbone was broken.

One of the men pulled the door shut, the other dragged her on. She followed without resistance, some of her anger toward Spike slipping.

Chapter Six

Spike kicked the wall in frustration, the movement sending sharp pain through his side. He had trained for this. He had to focus on that. He knew what was going to happen, and he was strong enough to take it. But was Abigail? Damn. He wished to hell for the hundredth time, the thousandth, that he hadn't dragged her into this.

She hated him. The words shouldn't have hurt. They shouldn't have mattered. And yet they did.

He shut her picture out of his mind and focused on their predicament instead. Pain pulsated through him. Being prepared for something like this was one thing; being in captivity for real was something else entirely. A first for him. He knew plenty of guys who had been there and made it through. And plenty who hadn't.

Brian Welkins. He'd gone through his FBI training with Welkins, a good guy with a heart as big and open as Montana, the state from which he hailed. They'd gotten along pretty well, become friends. Welkins had saved his life with quick thinking when that bomb blew and cracked Spike's head. He'd never gotten to repay the debt. Brian Welkins had disappeared on his very first SDDU mission, almost four years ago now. Had he ended up in a place like this? How long had he stayed alive, hanging in there without any hope of rescue? Welkins had been one tough son of a bitch and had probably fought to the bitter end. Spike stiffened. And so would he.

He recalled the others they'd lost through the years. The job wasn't without its hazards. Special Forces suffered fifteen times more casualties on average than regular troops. He refused to become part of the statistics. He wasn't fighting only for himself. He fought to honor those who'd gone before. He fought for Abigail.

And she sure was worth fighting for.

What she was doing in Tukatar, the kids, the fire in her eyes. He'd do anything, kill anyone, to make sure she didn't lose that.

The door opened suddenly. He hated that—how he was still half-deaf from the explosion and couldn't hear them approach. The light came on and blinded him.

"One of you has to tell me what's going on," Suhaib said. "If you answer my questions, I won't have to ask your wife again."

He could see others standing behind him. Three men. "There's nothing to tell."

Using prisoners against each other was the oldest interrogation technique in the book. Whatever he told

Jamal would have little effect on how they treated Abigail. The decision to kill them both had been made when they were brought here. Suhaib could not afford to let them go.

"Who sent you?" he asked.

"I'm from the Barnsley Foundation."

The man shook his head and walked out, leaving him with the three thugs.

Damn. They were going to beat him again. He curled up to protect his vital organs.

The first kick hit his kidney and made him see honest-to-goodness stars. He didn't fight back this time, didn't want them to know that he still had strength left. If they wanted to kill him they would have shot him in the head. But it seemed the plan was to beat him unconscious a couple of times a day until they wore him down.

He took the abuse, not bothering to hold back his groans. Then he went limp and let his head fall back. The men stopped after a few more kicks. He heard the metal door bang against its frame as it closed behind them.

Hard to breathe.

He lay without moving until the pain abated to a bearable level. He would have given anything to know what was happening to Abigail. And they left him a long time to wonder—all night. Another tactic. He would not allow himself to think of all the horrid things she might be suffering. He focused every ounce of energy he had on exploring all possible avenues of escape.

They had found the camp. He had to let the Colonel know the location before it was too late. He could not let the operation fail, and he could not let El Jafar suspect just how much the U.S. already had on him. Abigail knew nothing, so they couldn't get information out of her. His cell phone had a couple of numbers programmed in, not to mention a few special functions, but they couldn't access those without a code. And he would die before he would talk.

Which didn't sound half-bad right about now. There was no pain in death. Resting pain-free in the cool sand sounded damn appealing. The temperature could be twenty or thirty degrees cooler just a few feet down. Of course, he'd probably get a shallow grave, if any. He pushed away the momentary temptation to give up. He couldn't die. If he did, Abigail was sure to die with him.

And so would countless others.

ABIGAIL SAT on the floor and watched the small hole on the opposite wall, about two inches wide and maybe four inches long. The strip of sunshine on the floor beneath it kept appearing and disappearing. Someone was out there moving around. Probably a guard.

The door was locked. She'd tried it. No way to escape.

Her only hope of getting out of there alive was if Spike somehow found a way, or if his supervisors figured out where they were and sent a team to get them.

She hoped he'd been in close touch with his boss. But, of course, even if their captors let them see each other again, she couldn't very well ask him.

Something poked in through the hole but disappeared before she could see what it was. Had Spike gotten out? Hope rushed through her. There it was again, a thin thing with a little knob on the end—gone as fast as it appeared. Maybe one of those flextube spy minicameras she'd seen in movies. She got up and moved closer. Spike's people had come for him. They were saved.

She stopped at the hole and bent down, considered sticking her finger through it. "I'm in here," she whispered. "I need help."

There it was again.

A scorpion!

She jumped up as the animal scuttled in and backed away from it as far as the small cell allowed, goose bumps covering her from head to toe. She hated creepy crawly things.

The scorpion came in a foot or so. She was ready to climb the walls. She was barefoot and had nothing to defend herself with. What the hell was the damn thing doing there? It was the middle of the day. They were supposed to sleep under rocks in the heat and forage for food at night. It had been one of the first things she'd learned upon arrival to Tukatar—to always check her shoes in the morning.

The nasty thing skittered toward the wall. She

moved, too, to keep the largest possible distance between them at all times. She tried to calm herself with the thought that scorpions were probably scared of people. Few animals attacked without being provoked.

She mirrored its movements as the scorpion ran along the perimeter of the room. She had to get rid of it. Now. She glanced at the hole. If one came in, so could another. That freaked her out so badly she couldn't even think about it.

She took off her veil and moved toward the animal, bent at the waist, and standing as far from him as possible, lowered the end of the cloth to the ground in front of him. The animal backed away from the black material. Excellent. All she had to do was to herd the damn thing outside.

For an insane moment she felt infinitely grateful to her captors that they had left her light on. Spike had been in the dark. She shuddered at the thought of that happening to her, scorpions crawling over her body.

She shooed the animal back, but it bolted sideways. She jumped away, her heart clamoring in her chest. Scorpions and humans had coexisted in these regions for thousands of years, she told herself. It didn't make an iota of difference to her frantic mind.

She had to get it out.

She moved forward, pushing the veil toward the animal. It stared at the cloth. Would it attack? She stopped. The scorpion backed away. Toward the hole, thank God. She took a cautious step. The scorpion skittered back to the wall. Almost at the hole. Her hands trembled. Just a little more. She shook the veil and, holding her breath, watched the animal back out of the room. She jammed the cloth in the hole with trembling hands, blocking it from any other intruder, and sank into the farthest corner.

She was breathing heavily, her blood rushing through her veins, the picture of the nasty thing still in front of her. Rubbing her arms didn't help. She seemed to have permanent goose bumps.

She cringed when she heard footsteps outside the door. They couldn't possibly interrogate her again. Not now. She couldn't take it. She had had all that she could bear for one day.

When the door opened, the man who came in didn't grab her, but set a plate of food and a flask of water on the floor instead. He stared at her hair, the veil jammed into the hole in the wall, but he didn't say anything as he left.

She fell on the food, starving all of a sudden, as if her body were just now remembering how hungry it was. She could barely taste the round noodles and sauce as she shoveled the meal down, breaking only for greedy swallows of water now and then. Then it was gone, too soon, and she felt slightly sick to her stomach. She'd eaten too fast.

She lay down, pressed a hand to her abdomen. After a while, the nausea passed. They'd given her food. The significance of it hit her finally. They wanted to keep her alive, at least for a while yet. A day or two? More? Hopefully long enough for someone to figure out where Spike and she had disappeared to and to come get them. She didn't want to die. Not this way. Not here.

"WHAT DO THEY say?" El Jafar tapped his gold-ringed finger on the desk.

"Nothing."

He nodded. "I think the woman is just a pawn, but Thornton—he wasn't in that cellar by accident."

"We'll get him to talk."

"Do." He shot the man a level look. "Then get rid of them. I want no trace left of either one."

"It will be done."

"By tomorrow night. I'm going to need every man. I don't want the distraction of prisoners. I can't spare enough people to guard them."

The man bowed and backed out of the room.

Damn the Americans. He tapped his fingers on the desk. How much did they know about him? It couldn't be a lot. He'd gone to extraordinary measures on security. He'd been careful. The two at camp were an irritation, but hardly a threat to him. He worried more about the ones who had sent them.

What had "Gerald Thornton" seen at the house, and had he been able to report back any of it? He would have given anything to know. Allah willing, his men would get the answers from the prisoners. They knew what they were doing and were not the squeamish kind.

THE DOOR opened. Spike pulled up his knees to protect himself and watched as a guard shoved Abigail into the room. This time, the man turned the light on. Probably so Spike could see the pitiful shape she was in. She looked thinner than ever, her hair unruly—she had lost her veil. Her eyes were swimming in tears. Damn. She looked like she was at the end of her rope.

The door slammed closed and they were alone.

"Hang in there," he said, feeling like a bastard.

The look she shot him told him she was of the same opinion. She was trembling slightly, her nerves and her body pushed to the edge.

He had to calm her down, distract her, boost her spirits somehow. If he found a way to escape, she had to be ready and strong enough in both body and spirit to go with him.

"Tell me about Uganda."

She looked at him as if not comprehending his words. But then, after a while, the clouds cleared from her eyes and she nodded.

"I was there with the Peace Corps."

"Working with war orphans?" He knew what she'd been working on, but wanted to get her talking.

"Some, but not all of them. I worked with young women who escaped from or were returned by the rebels. A lot of young people had been captured and taken into slavery."

He waited, hoping she would go on.

"I helped them locate their families, worked with the

local governments. Just talked to them. Tried to make them understand that what happened to them was not their fault, that their families still loved them and wanted them back. They'd survived terrible abuse."

"Some of the strongest people I've met in my life are women. If you don't lose hope, you can survive anything," he said, relieved when she nodded at his words.

"We held some classes, too. I taught English, another woman from Michigan gave sewing lessons. We got a dozen sewing machines donated. They had this amazing spirit. Both the volunteers and the girls." A little bit of spark returned to her eyes. "Like anything was possible."

"Weren't you scared? It's not the safest of countries."

She pulled her lips into a flat smile. "I was frightened out of my mind every single day. I'm such a coward. I kept expecting that the government would be overthrown again and we'd be all murdered in our beds."

"But you stuck with it."

"How could I not? I couldn't leave them."

"And then you came here."

"I found out about the grant from the Barnsley Foundation, that they wanted to do something in Beharrain. I did a little research and what I found... I don't know." She looked away. "It just broke my heart."

"And then you came. Alone."

She blew out a puff of air. "That decision might have been a little too rash."

Yeah. It had sure sent the CIA scampering. He

grinned despite the pain that even the small movement caused. "You're going to be fine."

She looked at him and slowly squared her shoulders, as if pulling strength from deep within. She was the most extraordinary woman he'd ever met.

"You promise?" she asked, holding his gaze.

He reached for her hand, ignoring the pain, savoring the feel of her fingers intertwined with his. She didn't pull away.

He took a deep breath. "Promise."

He'd break them out of there or die trying.

HE PROMISED. And she wanted to believe him. But considering that most everything that had come out of his mouth since they'd met had been a lie, it wasn't easy.

The door banged open and four men came in. One of them pulled her up by the arm and led her out. The others stayed with Spike. She had a pretty good idea what they were going to do to him.

He looked as if he'd been beaten savagely. She wondered how much more he could take.

The guard led her down the hall, then outside. She held her breath as they walked past the largest of the buildings where she knew the electrodes waited. She didn't dare breathe until they were past it, heading toward the smaller structure that contained her cell.

The man opened the door, shoved her inside. His eyes stopped on her veil, stuffed into the hole in the wall. He grabbed it and threw it at her. She did not protest, but covered her head, said nothing about the scorpion. If they knew she was scared of them, for sure they'd use that against her.

He left without a word, but she wasn't alone long. The young man who'd questioned her before walked into the cell. Her spirits sunk. He was bad news. Although he'd never hit her, when pain had come, it'd been always on his order. She cringed away from him, pressing her body into the far corner.

"Dr. Abigail DiMatteo. You say you came here to save children." He watched her face closely. "Are you a spy?"

"No," she said, although she knew he wouldn't believe her. "I'm not a spy. I don't know how to convince you."

He sucked in his lower lip, let it go. "Your husband is."

"I don't know anything about this. We've only just met."

"In my country, men would protect their families with their lives. They do not put them in danger."

She hung her head, having no idea where this was going.

"You don't have to die with him." His voice was nonthreatening, even friendly.

"I don't know anything," she said to the floor.

"I'll come back in a little while. Maybe you remember. I hope you will. Hamid is going to help you."

He walked out the door, gave some orders outside,

presumably to Hamid. She eyed with apprehension the stocky man who came in a minute later. He carried a three-foot steel chain in his scarred hands. Her stomach contracted into a hard ball at the sight.

He grabbed her roughly by her bound wrists and dragged her out of the room and out of the building. She stumbled after him. Fear—hot, visceral panic—flooded her body and mind. Then her thoughts cleared somewhat. Should she fight him? Her gaze settled on the chain. He could do considerably more damage to her than she could do to him. But she had to try something. She threw her weight back, trying to stop the man.

He yanked hard on her wrists in response, the ropes bruising her skin. She struggled despite the pain. He didn't even slow. She fought on, dragging her weight, pulling back. He was taking her away from the buildings, outside the giant camouflage netting that stretched over them.

She had to close her eyes for a moment when they stepped out into the full sun, its merciless rays blinding as they reflected off the white sand. The bottom of her feet burned. "Stop, please, stop," she said in her best Arabic. "I didn't do anything."

Hamid walked on. She could see his destination now, a tall post dug into the sand about ten yards in front of them. She struggled harder, putting all her strength into it, but he pulled her along as easily as if she were a child.

When they reached the post, he threaded the chain through the loop of her tied arms, then yanked her wrists high above her head and slipped the ends of the chain onto a thick nail driven in the post at an angle.

"You speak, get water," he said in heavily accented English and, with a last look at his handiwork, left her tied out in the full sun.

She wondered how long it'd be before he came back to see if the heat had broken her resistance yet, and hoped he didn't overestimate her and she'd be still alive.

The soles of her feet burned on the hot sand. She dug in a few inches to find relief in the cooler layer beneath, bent her head forward, making sure the sun didn't reach the unprotected skin of her face. The black *abayah* soaked up the heat. Her mouth was already as dry as the desolate landscape around her. How long would it be before her tongue began to swell? Her wrists hurt where the rope cut into her skin. She straightened her spine to stand taller and ease the pull of the chain. She felt marginally better, but how long could she keep that up?

How long before the sun sucked out the last of her strength?

Chapter Seven

Steel scraped against cement. Spike opened his left eye and tried forcing open the right, but couldn't make it work. It was still swollen shut. A guard entered the cell, making him instinctively curl up on the floor, tuck his head in and prepare himself psychologically for the beating. His body was strong, his mind ready; he could take it. They could not break him. He waited.

Something clinked against the floor, then the door closed and he was alone again. He let his muscles relax as he looked around, his eyes settling on a small metal bowl of unrecognizable food and a goatskin water pouch by the wall. He inched over and smiled, just as wide as his cracked lips allowed. This was what he'd been waiting for—a single mistake he could take advantage of. And they had finally made one.

The strap had been removed from the water pouch and they didn't give him a spoon—smart precautions, but not enough. He drank first, then ate, enough adrenaline rushing through his veins to dull the pain of chewing. When both the food and water were gone, he dragged himself into the far corner and sat with his back to the door.

He scraped the edge of the bowl against the rough concrete. It didn't seem to make much of a noise, but he couldn't be sure. His hearing was far from recovered. He waited a few minutes and when no one came in, continued. Soon enough, the bowl's edge was sufficiently sharp to cut the rope; but the cutting itself, the slow sawing of fibers, took time. He worked on his feet first, then his hands, not severing the ropes completely but enough so that a good tug would finish them. He didn't cut in the middle, but instead on the inside of his left wrist, to make the damage as unnoticeable as he could.

When he was done, he turned the bowl over and pushed it into the corner, the sharpened edge hidden, then he lay down to wait. He didn't have to wait long before Suhaib entered the room, along with another man who was dragging Abigail behind him. Two more guys came in. They pulled Spike from the floor. Every movement hurt, and he let it show, refusing to lock his knees to stand. Let them think he was too weak to hold up himself.

He lifted his head enough to take a good look at Abigail, gritted his teeth as he damned the bastards to hell. She looked worse than before, weak, on the brink of giving up. Fear filled her eyes. And she didn't even know what was coming. He did. Another favorite interrogation technique—they were going to torture her in front of him.

Two men held him by one wall, while Abigail was led to the opposite corner. Suhaib paced the room but a few feet from her, a handgun tucked into his belt.

"I've been very patient with you," he addressed his words to Spike. "But I'm afraid we're running out of time. I'm going to ask you one more time who sent you. If you choose to lie again, your wife will pay the price." The man stopped in front of Abigail.

He could not reach Suhaib in one leap from where he was and didn't dare risk the man pulling the gun.

"I already told you everything I know," he said, hoping to provoke the man into moving closer to him.

Instead, Suhaib pulled a curved dagger from his belt and lay the blade against Abigail's throat.

"No," Spike roared, but even as he did, the man hooked the dagger into the front of her clothes and sliced down to her waist, baring her skin for all to see.

He was going to rape her.

Rage welled, pumping through Spike's veins, pushing him to jump, choke, pummel. He held back. Not yet. Not yet. If Suhaib moved just two steps in his direction…

Abigail struggled against the man who held her, slipped an arm free and elbowed him hard in the stomach. Suhaib swore, then pulled his gun and placed the barrel against her temple.

They had pushed Suhaib too far. "Wait," Spike yelled, and lurched forward, hard enough to make the guards holding him pay attention, but not strong enough to break free.

They threw him back against the wall, as he had expected. He let his head hit. "I work for the United States government," he mumbled as he rolled his eyes back and slowly slid to the floor, then went completely limp.

Suhaib swore again.

Pain exploded in Spike's ribs when somebody kicked him, but he didn't move, not even when they threw water into his face.

Then he heard the words he had been hoping for. "Get me when he comes to." The door opened and closed.

He waited a good fifteen minutes, giving Suhaib time to get out of hearing distance before he stirred without opening his eyes. One of the guards bent over him, blocking the light. The next second his hands were on the man's head, his ropes dangling, as he smashed the man's skull into the concrete floor with full force. He kicked the legs out from under the other guy simultaneously, then he was on his feet, his heel crushing the man's windpipe in one good kick.

The guard holding Abigail went for his gun, but it was too late. Spike was on him in a split second. With his ears still ringing, he didn't even hear the guy's neck snap.

Abigail stared at him with wide-eyed horror, trembling, grabbing for the front of her clothes to hold the fabric together.

"Are you okay?" he asked as he searched the bodies.

His search yielded two knives and three guns. Not bad. He cut her ropes, handed her one of the guns. It slipped from her fingers, her hand was shaking so badly.

"Let's go." He swung the straps of his two rifles over his shoulder, picked up hers and kept it at the ready.

She didn't move. He grabbed her hand and pulled her behind him. They had no time to wait until she came out of shock. He found the narrow hall empty and windowless, but riddled with enough bullet holes to see through. Only a couple of men were outside, the heat already merciless.

He turned to Abigail, rage bubbling up inside him again. They'd done a number on her. He made sure his voice was soft when he spoke. "Where did they keep you?"

"In a small cell."

"Here?"

She shook her head.

Excellent. That meant she'd been outside. "Have you seen any trucks?"

She thought about that for a moment. "They're behind the main building."

"How close?"

"I don't know." Her gaze finally focused on him. "A hundred yards."

He pulled her back into his cell, stripped one of the men and put on his uniform, taking the headdress and wrapping it around his own head to cover up his blond hair. When he was done, he took the other two kaffiyehs, folded them then wrapped them around Abigail's bare feet.

"Keep your hands together at the wrist."

She seemed reluctant to let her clothes go.

"Here." He removed her hand, pulled on the material of the *abayah* and tied it at the neck. The black fabric still gaped in the middle. He salvaged a length of rope and bound it below her breasts. That held. "We have to go." He grabbed her arm, led her from the cell and then from the building.

The men were a good three hundred yards away. One of them yelled out. Abigail looked back at him, her eyes filled with panic. Spike pushed her forward roughly, mumbling "sorry" under his breath. Another man yelled, but not at them, Spike realized after a moment.

"Don't look at them," he whispered, as he searched the camp without turning his head. He spotted two ancient army Jeeps on the other side of the training court and filed that information as backup.

He walked as if taking her to the main building, ducking behind it at the last second. Four trucks lined the sand in front of him. He couldn't have planned it better. He walked to the one that held a row of gas cans in the back, determined not to make the same mistake twice. He didn't want to get stranded in the middle of the desert again due to lack of fuel.

"Get in and get down." He pushed her up into the cab and breathed a sigh of relief when she soundlessly obeyed.

He didn't tarry long, just enough to slash the tires on the rest of the vehicles. He was in the driver's seat and had the truck hotwired within seconds. Then they were flying across the sand. The first shots rang out just a few seconds later.

"Stay down," he said, keeping his eyes on the terrain before them, not wanting to flip over the truck on a sand dune.

She looked at him, myriad emotions flashing across her face. Determination was the last and it stuck. She grabbed one of the rifles, leaned out the window and returned fire.

Dr. Abigail DiMatteo, peace activist. He grinned. He could get used to having her around.

He got a good head start, but it wasn't long before the two army Jeeps appeared behind them. The lighter vehicles, which were easier to drive on the sand, were catching up. Whoever was riding in them had good guns, big ones. Sooner or later they were bound to hit one of the gas cans in the back and blow the truck to kingdom come. Spike slammed on the brakes and turned the truck so he faced their pursuers head-on. He lifted a rifle out the window. Between him and Abigail, it didn't take long to pick off the men.

"Are you okay?" He glanced at her as he put the truck in gear again.

"Fine. Are we safe?"

She was speaking at last. A good sign.

"For now." He had a feeling they hadn't seen the last of El Jafar's men.

Eager to put distance between the terrorist camp and themselves, he drove as fast as was safely possible, paying attention to the position of the sun and trying to figure out which way Tihrin was. He wished they hadn't taken his watch and cell phone.

"So you work for the government." Her voice cracked.

He glanced at her, then back at the sand that stretched before them. "Yes."

She took a deep breath. "You could have given me a warning."

"No, I really couldn't have."

She closed her eyes for a moment and shook her head. "Now what?"

"We'll find the nearest phone and call in the location of the camp."

"That's what you've been after from the beginning." She sounded tired, resigned.

He owed her some explanation. "I was supposed to recruit you, but at the end there was no time."

They rode on in silence.

"So the foundation money was bogus?" she asked after a while, then her eyes widened. "The call. In hindsight, it makes perfect sense."

"I don't know a lot about that part. I came in later."

"I got a call from someone at the foundation, saying they were establishing a new grant for work with children in war-torn countries, and they would like to see something done in Beharrain, since it's gotten so little foreign aid so far. The woman who called said they had read the article I wrote about my work in Uganda and would be delighted if I submitted a grant proposal. I thought it was strange, because one of the girls I went to Uganda with works for the Barnsley Foundation now and we keep in touch and she hadn't said anything about a new grant."

"I wouldn't be surprised if they made it up just for you."

"Why me? Why was I picked? Jamal came in contact with a bunch of people at the university."

"I'm sure all of them were looked at. I think they had other candidates at the beginning, but you seemed the strongest. You had a history of working in a situation similar to Beharrain. They knew Jamal would remember the kind of stuff you were into in college. You had built-in credibility. You are a woman, less suspicious or threatening than a man. You're athletic. You were on the biathlon team, so they knew you weren't scared of guns. You weren't the perfect candidate, but, all things considered, you were pretty damn good. Good enough for the CIA to hedge their bets on."

"Excuse me if I'm not flattered."

He simply shrugged. "Why did you leave early? You were supposed to be evaluated, recruited and trained before you left the U.S. You didn't wait for the grant award to be announced."

"After I told my girlfriend about the grant, she asked around about it. And then a while later, she saw my name on the paperwork and accidentally found out I won. I was going through a rough time in my personal life. She told me the good news to cheer me up. I needed to get away and I had some funds set aside, so I figured I'd leave early and start setting up."

"You put your own money into this?"

"I'd been saving for something else that fell through."

"Another project?"

"Something like that," she repeated his evasive words back to him.

Okay, so she didn't want to talk. He could wait her out.

"A wedding," she said finally when she'd apparently grown uncomfortable with the silence.

There'd been a copy of a marriage license in her CIA file, but no marriage certificate. He'd wondered about that. "You left him?" He couldn't imagine a man who would willingly leave her.

"Damn right." Anger gave strength to her voice. "So your people are looking for us? Leave no man behind, right?"

"Not really." He hated to bring her down but didn't want to give her false hope. It'd be better if she knew it was all up to them. "My team works on the if-you-get-caught-we'll-deny-we've-ever-heard-of-you principle."

She sucked in a deep breath then exhaled. "Don't overwhelm me with all the good news at once."

She was all right. Maintaining a sense of humor

under the kind of stress they were in showed amazing strength. "The real good news is we're going to make it out of here."

Her face grew serious. "You think so?"

"Piece of cake," he said.

SHE WAS SLEEPING. Good. She needed rest to regain her strength. Spike turned his attention back to the rippling sand spread before them, which reflected the heat in waves. With both windows down, plenty of air moved through the truck's cab as he drove, but unfortunately it was hot air. Still, it made things bearable, as did the shade provided by the roof. The minor comforts had allowed them to drive through the worst of the day without stopping for shelter. They should have an easier time now that the sun had passed its zenith and was on its way to the horizon.

He glanced at the dashboard, at the little needle resting on red. They were out of gas. He had hoped it would last a while, not wanting to wake Abigail. The motor coughed a couple of times. They weren't going to make it much farther without refueling. He turned the truck at an angle to make sure she had as much shade on her as possible, then stopped.

She opened her eyes as soon as the truck ceased moving.

"Gotta fill up the tank. Might as well stretch your legs."

She sat up straight in her seat and looked around, disappointment clear on her face. She'd probably thought they'd reached Tihrin.

"It won't be long now." He opened the door and jumped onto the sand, swore at the pain in his side as he walked around to help her out.

She slipped a little, ending up sliding down against him, which he would have enjoyed tremendously under different circumstances. As it was, they both winced in pain.

The corner of his mouth tugged up. "We are a sorry pair." He steadied her and walked to the back.

She followed after him.

They had six cans of gasoline, more than enough to get to Tihrin even if they made an accidental detour, although he wasn't planning on that. The desert lay to the south of the city. As long as they drove north, they should hit a populated area. The ride out to camp had taken about eight hours, so the ride back should be the same. And he could chart their position by the stars easier than by the sun, so nightfall shouldn't slow them down. He didn't think Tihrin was all that far off, but the going was slow over the uneven terrain and loose sand.

He lifted a five-gallon green metal can off the back of the truck, biting back a groan when pain pulsated through his side. He ignored it as he twisted off the cap and lifted the can to the tank. Some of the gasoline sloshed on his sandals—except it didn't smell like gasoline at all. He sniffed the can, poured some of its contents into the palm of his hand. Water. It sure came in handy. He tasted it. Warm, but clean, drinkable water. That was one less thing he needed to worry about.

"Would you like a drink?" He offered the can to Abigail, who was coming around the truck, then poured some into her hands and twisted the cap back on when she was done. He lifted the can into the back, climbed up and opened another one. Water. Another, another, another. They were all the same.

"Damn."

"What?"

"We don't have any gas." He climbed down.

"Right here is the reason most people in Tukatar own camels." She plopped on the sand but got up after a few seconds.

"Too hot?" He came over and pushed aside the top few inches of sand to get to the cooler layer below, creating a bench-sized area. He sat down next to her, needing a little time to think. "There's probably enough oil below us to fuel all the cars in the country."

"Life is full of irony." She poked her fingers into the sand. "Shouldn't we start walking?"

"Not yet." It had to be well over a hundred degrees. They wouldn't get far. "We'll rest until the sun goes down, then walk at night. It's better to keep moving once the temperature drops anyway."

"Desert survival training?" She smiled at him for the first time in a long time.

He grinned back. "Comes in handy now and then."

They climbed into the back where the canvas kept

out the sun overhead. He flipped up the two sides to let some of the breeze in, positioned the water cans at the back as a makeshift barricade, just in case, and made sure they had all three rifles with them.

He settled in, sitting up to make sure he could see. Abigail did the same.

"You should stretch out. Make yourself comfortable."

She was staring at his face. "Is your cheekbone broken?"

He touched the swollen flesh and winced. "I don't think so."

She got up, took off her veil and soaked it in water, then came back to put it on his face. "What else did they do to you?"

"I think I might have a couple of broken ribs." Not that he was a complainer, but it didn't seem all that bad to have her fuss over him.

"Let me bind them up." She began to tear strips off her *abayah*, revealing her ankles and then her calves through the flimsy nightgown she wore underneath.

He didn't stop her.

"Lie down." She knelt next to him.

He shook his head. "I want to keep an eye on things."

She went still for a moment then glanced back over her shoulder into the direction they'd come from.

Damn. He didn't want her to worry. "I think we have some time. It'll take a while before they catch up with us. Pray for wind." They needed that more than anything to erase their tracks from the sand.

She looked back at him and reached for his shirt, her slender fingers working their way down the buttons efficiently. Her breasts, eye level to him, rose and fell with each breath. He felt his blood stir, looked away. When she was finished with the buttons, she moved the shirt out of the way and ran her fingers down his ribs, gently probing one after another. His body didn't seem to know its own limits. He dropped his hands into his lap, not wanting to embarrass her.

"That one," he said when she got to one of the spots that hurt like hell.

She nodded and moved on. They identified three broken ribs on the left and two on the right before she was finished.

"It's terrible." Her voice shook with upset.

"Could be worse. At least none of them punctured my lungs."

She stared at him for a few seconds. "I don't even want to think about that." Her hands trembled slightly.

Exhaustion and the shock of the last couple of days were probably catching up with her. He couldn't let her fall apart now. "I'm sorry, but it looks like you'll have to take care of me for a couple of days. You think you can handle it?"

She drew a deep breath then nodded. "Sit up."

He'd given her a challenge and she took it up. Good. Now she had something to focus on, to take her mind off other things she could be worried about. He leaned away from the back of the truck toward her, his face inches from her breasts. She'd been right. Life *was* full of irony. He'd wanted to distract her, and here he was, himself severely distracted.

She leaned closer still, to wrap strips of cloth around his torso. She tugged the makeshift bandage tight. Strangely, he didn't seem to feel any pain.

"Good as new." She moved away too soon. "Wish we had some painkillers."

He leaned back and looked her in the eye. "You could kiss me."

He'd caught her off guard. Her eyes widened before she quickly glanced away. "Listen, back at the house—I don't want you to think I—"

"It's good to give thinking a break every once in a while." He reached for her. "If I thought about it, I probably wouldn't do this." He pulled her to him and kissed her.

Her lips were soft beneath his and they parted as she relaxed in his arms. She felt like heaven. He deepened the kiss, taking it all, wanting more. She was like a sandstorm—she came up on him fast, spun his mind around, blinded him.

She felt it, too. He could tell from the small sound that escaped her throat, the way her breath caught when he pushed his hardness against her. But just as he was getting good and lost in her, she stiffened and pulled away. Damn. That was the trouble with women. They couldn't stop thinking. Couldn't let the tide wash them away wherever it may, to hell with the consequences. He knew what was coming before she opened her mouth.

"Do you always take whatever you want, the minute you want it, without any thought to others?"

Only when it came to women, although not without any thought to them. He'd always made sure they had as much fun as he did. Nobody had ever complained. "Not usually."

"Good to know I'm special." She settled down on the truck bed, as far from him as possible, and pulled her knees up. "If you think I'd forgotten all that lying, you better think again."

The *abayah* slid up her thighs, her sheer nightgown revealing slender limbs. He forced his gaze to move up and away from that trouble spot. Not that her swollen lips were less tempting. And he was willing to bet anything the flush on her cheeks had nothing to do with righteous indignation.

He turned the other way. "The whole point of a covert operation is that it's done without anyone knowing. I didn't have the time to evaluate you to see if you could handle it. Would you have been able to keep your silence with Suhaib?"

"Who?"

He turned back to her. "El Jafar. Jamal's brother."

"Oh."

He could see the wheels turning in her head.

"We didn't run into Jamal by accident," she said.

He shook his head.

"So the fire at the hut..."

"I made sure you were safe. It was the only way I could think of to get you to Tihrin in a hurry."

"And the explosion?"

"They caught me snooping in the armory." He went on and explained the original plan, then the adjusted one and how it had gone wrong. "Look, the world is changing. It's not countries against countries anymore. Our enemy is not a traditional army. We can't just draw the front line on a map and talk strategy about how to push it forward. A surgical operation like this works best against a small target. Would you rather have the whole U.S. Army come in and bomb guilty and innocent alike?"

She gave him a dark look. "I still hate it."

"I know. I had no right to put your life at risk."

"If you had told me, I would have volunteered."

She probably would have. Unfortunately, he hadn't known her well enough to make that judgment call, and he hadn't wanted to go against a direct order. But when he looked at the rope burns on her wrists, the knowledge that he'd done the best he could didn't keep him from feeling like a bastard.

ABIGAIL WOKE to the touch of his hand on her shoulder, sore but feeling much better after finally having gotten enough sleep.

"Time to go," he said. "Are you okay?"

She looked at him, outlined against the sky, larger

than life. Right now, at this moment, he was the only thing standing between her and certain death. And maybe he was the only thing standing between a lot of other people and death, too. She hated his methods, but at the same time understood him. The stakes were enormous. He had to do whatever it took.

The sun was low in the sky, preparing to dip below the horizon. She stood, her limbs stiff from having slept on the hard wood. "How do you feel?"

He flashed a grin. "Like hell. But I've been worse."

The left side of his face had turned a sickening shade of purple. He jumped off the truck, and she took the hand he offered her.

"Water?" He lifted off one of the cans. "We can wash, too. There's no way to take all this with us."

She held out her palms and drank deeply, used to drinking warm water by now. When she had enough, she threw some into her face. It felt like heaven.

"How would you like a shower?"

She glanced at him. Was he serious? Wasting so much water seemed like sacrilege. And then it hit her. They were lost in the middle of the desert. On foot. It seemed impossible that they'd just be able to walk out. If they stayed with the truck—shelter and water—the terrorists would find them. In any case, the water wouldn't last forever. If they walked, they could only take a few cans with them. And of course, she remembered suddenly, they had no food. He was just trying to give her some relief before the end came.

He climbed back on the truck and lifted the can over her head. She untied the rope, pulled off the *abayah*, threw it in the back of the truck then hesitated.

"Go ahead. I won't look."

She had nothing on but her panties under the flimsy, ripped nightgown. Oh, what the hell. They were going to die anyway. With her back to him, she grabbed the hem and pulled the thing off.

The gentle trickle of water felt like heaven on her skin. He circled with the can above her head to make sure he got all of her. Too soon, the water was gone.

"Thank you." She tried to reach for her clothes without turning.

"One more." He dumped another can of water just on her hair, rinsing it completely.

She could have kissed him.

"Your turn," she said instead, and quickly dressed, putting the *abayah* on backward to cover her front.

He helped her up into the truck bed, her fingers and palm tingling where they touched. She let go of him at once. When their eyes met, the heat in his took her breath away. Then he turned her around and tied the *abayah* in the back so it would stay in place. When he was done, he jumped onto the sand with easy grace, despite his injuries. She squatted to twist the cap off a can, had a little trouble, but managed without his help. She lifted the can and turned, then stopped, rooted to the spot.

He'd taken off everything but the bandages.

He stood facing away from her, probably for her

sake more than out of modesty, his wide shoulders tapering to narrow hips, below which the most magnificent male ass that ever existed demanded her attention.

"Whenever you're ready," he said in a suggestive tone, and she nearly fell off the truck.

She lifted the can and tilted it. The water hit the sand so she adjusted, following its way with her eyes as it poured over his body. He had a beautiful physique, despite the two old bullet wounds—one on his left shoulder, the other above the right hip. If she were a better woman, she would have looked away instead of ogling for all she was worth.

"One more?" She croaked the words past her suddenly dry throat when the water ran out.

"That would be nice."

She poured the second can faster, embarrassed by her lack of control and turned when the water ran out, to give him privacy to dress. He helped her off the truck when he was done, then pulled his knife and began to cut the thick canvas of the truck.

"What's that for?"

"You're going to need something more substantial for your feet."

What was the point? They had about as much chance as a snowman of walking out of the desert alive. But she appreciated his efforts to boost their spirits and how he wouldn't let on that they were doomed, no matter what they did.

Chapter Eight

Tsernyakov was a cunning man. He had not been there at the delivery. He'd sent only a half dozen men with the valuable cargo, all disposable. El Jafar rubbed his mustache. He hoped they were all disposable. If Tsernyakov was smart enough not to come himself, then he was probably smart enough to know not to send anyone important from his staff. The delivery crew had been taken care of. Which left Tsernyakov as the only outstanding issue.

Take him out before he became a liability or keep him in case his services were needed in the future? He grunted in impatience when one of his servants came in, bowing, interrupting his thoughts.

"What do you want?"

"There's a man at the door. He says he has a message from his sheik. Wouldn't say which one."

"Bring him in."

He poured himself a drink and drained it, then lit a cigar. He hadn't expected a messenger. Something had gone wrong. Allah willing, it was something minor. He'd forbidden all phone communication at this stage, not daring to risk detection. He was too close to victory to let anything or anyone get in his way now.

The servant brought a man in, then left, closing the door behind him.

The man, dressed in Bedouin clothes, bowed, his nervous fingers playing with his belt.

"You brought news?" El Jafar recognized him as one of the men from camp.

"The Americans escaped."

Hot fury flooded him as he reached into the drawer, his fingers finding the gun at once. Incompetent, worthless bastards, undisciplined ignorant bunch of idiots. Didn't they understand what was at stake? He pulled the gun, watched the man go pale and fall to his knees.

His men needed a lesson.

But not this lesson.

He set the gun on the table. There could be no gunshots heard from his house. He'd had a hard enough time explaining away the explosion. There should be nothing to draw attention now. After the attack, after he was a hero, more recruits would come, better ones, and plenty of funding to train them well. "They must be found."

"We have nearly every man out."

"I'll be there tonight. Go."

The man got on his feet, bowed deeply and left, no doubt thanking Allah for his merciful ways.

El Jafar picked up the gun and put it away. There had been too many mistakes. He would go to the camp tonight and tell them they were moving up the schedule.

ABIGAIL CARRIED two rifles; Spike had the third, plus a five-gallon can of water. It was all they needed, he'd said, and she hoped he was right. In any case, trying to carry more would have slowed them down too much.

They walked side by side under the cloudless starry sky, the desert like a vast blanket spreading before them. The going was not easy. They were in the dead lands now, which were nothing like the semiarid stretch between Tukatar and Rahmara. Here the loose sand was hard to walk in, and there wasn't a blade of grass or any other living thing in sight. They kept on all night, stopping briefly from time to time, resting no more than they absolutely had to. To her disappointment, the first ray of light revealed nothing but more sand on the horizon. The only thing interrupting the desert was a dark strip to their right, too small to be the city they were looking for.

Still, hope surged through her. "Do you think it's an oasis?"

"Can't tell yet," he said, but he changed direction slightly so that they would walk close enough by it to see.

By midmorning, they could identify the oddity, a rock ridge about twenty feet high and a half mile long, snaking in the sand. She hoped they would reach it within the hour and could spend the worst heat of the day in its shade. Having that goal, a visible destination in front of her, made walking easier. Unfortunately, an hour of exhausting effort later, the rocks seemed no closer.

"We need to rest." Spike stopped and dropped the water can on the sand.

"I'm not too bad. I can walk on until we reach the shade." She wanted that more than anything—to get away from the blazing sun for a little while.

"Not close enough. We need to conserve our energy." He drew a circle in the sand, stuck one of the rifle barrels down in the middle and examined its shadow as it fell on the circle.

Maybe he was getting loopy from the heat. "We could reach the rocks in an hour and rest in the shade. Can't be more than two miles," she said.

He glanced at her. "Try six or seven. Distances are about three times longer in the desert than what they seem to the naked eye. The flat sand and the way the sun reflects off it make judging tricky."

"Oh." She shrugged off the guns from her shoulder and propped them against the can. "Aren't we going to fry out here?" The temperature had to be above a hundred already and would easily reach one-twenty before the worst was over.

He stepped out of his sandals and handed one to her. "We better start digging."

She watched as he marked an area of six feet by three.

"We need to get down to about two or three feet. Pile

the sand on the long sides. It'll give us some extra protection from the sun."

They were going to make their own shade. It gave her hope, as well as something to do other than think about dying. She lowered herself to her knees and dug in. The loose sand was easy to scoop, but had the tendency of flowing back into place like water. She watched Spike's efficient, broad movements and tried to copy him, digging until her arms were sore, stopping only to drink then getting back to work again. The heat was nearly unbearable by the time they were done.

"Hop in and sit down," he said, then placed the water can and the rifles in the hole next to her.

He unwrapped his kaffiyeh. "Hang on to this end." He stretched the headdress over as much of the hole as it would cover, and anchored the edges with sand. He took off his shirt and did the same with that. About a third of the opening remained uncovered still.

She pulled the *abayah* over her head and handed it to him. He nodded, anchored one end, hopped into the hole and sat, pulling the material over his head and anchoring the other end to the side, scooping sand around the corners.

"As long as the wind doesn't pick up we should be fine. Lie down."

She did, surprised how much cooler the sand felt on the bottom, giving her much-needed relief from the heat. "It's nice," she said then fell silent as he stretched out next to her.

"Two or three feet can make a thirty-degree difference. You dig in a north-south direction, and the sand piled on the side gives some shade over the opening." He nodded to the assortment of garments above his head. "A cover helps, too."

Plenty of sunlight filtered through the clothes and gaps, but it was still much better than out there, where she could barely keep her eyes open, blinded from the sun as it reflected off the white sand. She appreciated the break. "How long are we staying?"

"Until late afternoon. Try to get some sleep." His face was too close, his gaze intent on her face.

She closed her eyes, so she wouldn't have to look into his. The narrow ditch didn't give them much room. Her hips and shoulders were touching him. "Do you think they're still looking for us?"

"We know their leader and saw the camp."

"Right." They weren't going to give up until she and Spike were dead. "Do you think they'll find us?"

"It's a big desert. They'd have to drive right over us to see us."

"Maybe once they find the truck, they'll think we'll die in the desert, anyway, so they won't bother looking."

"Maybe," he said. "But very unlikely."

She sighed and opened her eyes, finding him still looking at her. She appreciated that he treated her as an equal and for once told her the truth, as bad as it was.

"Can't afford to get lulled into some false sense of

security. We will both have to be on guard every minute to make it out alive," he said.

She looked away, up to the black *abayah* directly over her head, and all of a sudden she felt as if they were already in the grave. A shiver ran across her skin, fear filling her heart. All her old nightmares returned and rushed her with force, bringing with them forgotten terrors. She sat up, gasping for air.

"What is it?" Spike came up next to her.

"Nothing." Her heart beat out of control, pounding in her chest. "I think I'm having a panic attack." God, she hadn't had one in ages.

He put his arms around her and pulled her to him. After a while, she laid her head on his chest.

"Want to talk about it?"

She could hear his voice vibrate inside him, under her ear. "I'll be fine in a minute." She had no intention of sharing something so personal with him, but the words seemed to tumble out on their own. "When I was younger, I used to have nightmares about lying on the bottom of a grave. My sister died when I was eight."

He hugged her tighter.

"She was two years older than me. And it was like… I got so used to doing everything Kate did, only a little later. She lost her first tooth; two years later, I lost my first tooth. She went to kindergarten; two years later, I went to kindergarten. We had the same teachers, the same problems, only two years apart. Then when she got sick and died, I kept waiting for it to happen to me."

"It must have been terrible."

"I used to have these nightmares about my own funeral. Being on the bottom of the grave. Only I wasn't really dead, but for some reason I couldn't open my eyes or speak. And when I was awake I'd have panic attacks. Then a little after I passed the age when she died, they stopped."

His heart beat strong and steady under her cheek. She felt some of the tension ease from her body. "It's weird. I haven't thought about this in years."

"You've been under tremendous stress in the last couple of days. It's catching up with you, that's all. Stress and exhaustion."

"It's just that sometimes I still feel like I'm living on borrowed time."

He rested his chin on the top of her head and leaned back, taking her with him. They ended up lying together, his arm around her, her head resting on his shoulder. "Try to relax."

Unlikely. When she was a child, it used to take her hours to calm down after a panic attack. But then the next thing she knew, her eyes were closing and her worries floating away.

By the time she woke, the sun had passed its zenith. They must have slept a couple of hours. She didn't stir, not wanting to wake Spike, not ready to give up the comfort of his strong body just yet.

"Feeling better?" he asked.

"Can't believe I fell asleep again."

"Your body needs rest for healing."

He was right about that. Constantly blocking out the pain enough to go on took a lot of energy. And she had barely slept at the camp. First, she was too scared; then, they were waking her up all hours of the night to question her.

She glanced at him. He didn't look as if he had slept any. Come to think of it, the only time she had ever seen the man sleep was right after he had arrived in Tukatar. And boy, did that get her into trouble.

"We should start out," he said.

She moved away from him and sat up, a little embarrassed over what had happened earlier, grateful for the way he had handled it. "Thanks."

His blue eyes mesmerized her. She felt as if she were falling into his gaze, surrounded by it, embraced. He could have asked anything of her when he was looking at her like that and she would have done it. Thank God, he didn't know his own power.

"We should drink before we leave." He pulled the water can between them, breaking the connection.

She watched as he twisted off the cap and pushed the can toward her. She lifted it as she drank, the half-empty can lighter now. The lukewarm water felt good. She handed the can over to him and wiped her mouth, swallowing as he put his lips to the exact spot where hers had been a minute ago. He drank with his eyes closed, the strong muscles of his neck working with every swallow.

She began to stand, but he put a hand on her knee and pushed her back down.

"Let me take a look first." He twisted the cap back on, picked up one of the rifles, pulled the edge of his headdress from the sand and looked out. "We're fine." He stood, yanked the rest of the cloth free and helped her up.

She freed her *abayah* and pulled it over her head, covering her hair with the veil. He dressed, too, shrugging into his shirt, twisting the headdress around his head. The sun was low on the horizon, the air a good twenty degrees cooler than when they had stopped to rest.

"Are we still going to check out the rocks?" With the sun going down, they no longer needed their shade.

"Might as well. We might come upon a nest of scorpions. I could use some food. I was counting on having the truck and turning on the headlights once it got dark to catch the bugs it drew. Since we can't do that we'll have to find something else to eat."

If she wasn't sure he was only kidding, she would have gagged.

He picked up their water and his rifle. She slipped the other two guns over her shoulder. Amazing how much easier walking was without the sun beating down on them. It was a huge difference for her eyes, too. She didn't have to constantly squint.

They had nearly reached the shelter of the rocks when a strange sound seeped into the air from the east and began to grow.

"Trucks?" She looked at him, panicked.

The somber expression on his face did nothing to allay her fears. What little remained of the sunlight seemed to dim.

He stopped to listen for a few moments, then grabbed her hand and broke out in a dead run. "Sandstorm."

She put everything she had into it, her lungs burning, but she wasn't fast enough. The sandstorm was upon them in minutes, blinding them. The fast-flying sand felt harsh against her face, as if someone were trying to sandpaper her skin off. She could see nothing, so she squeezed her eyes shut to spare them and followed blindly as Spike pulled her forward.

"We have to reach shelter before the worst hits."

She could barely hear his words, which were blown away by the wind before they could fully reach her ears. She couldn't imagine this getting worse.

After an eternity, she tumbled into him. He'd stopped. They'd reached the cliff. She searched the stone wall for any indentation as they rounded it to get to the other side where the ridge would block some of the wind that was still growing in strength with every gust.

Her eyes, ears, nose and mouth were full of sand, small grains of it grinding between her teeth. She cupped her mouth to keep from more getting in and coughed. Spike pulled her forward and straightened her when she stumbled.

They reached a gap at last, more of a crevice than a cave, although it was big enough to allow both of them in. Spike crawled in first, reached the back at once and turned around. The place was just barely big enough for them to sit, with her practically on his lap, the ceiling too low to stand.

He brushed the sand from his face and she did the same, turning sideways so she could see him.

"How long do you think this will last?"

"No telling. Could be hours or days." He shrugged. "Nothing we can do about it. Damn." He shook his head. "I hoped we'd be able to cover some distance tonight."

She blinked, trying to get some of the sand out of her watering eyes without touching them with her dirty fingers. Things just seemed to get worse and worse, everything conspiring against them. Every time she felt the slightest ray of hope, something happened to set them back.

"Relax," he said, too close to her ear.

"I'm having a little trouble relaxing," she snapped at him. They were stuck in the desert in a sandstorm with nothing but a few gallons of water.

He cupped her face in his hands, his brilliant blue eyes shining in the dim cave.

"I'm not going to let anything happen to you. You know that, right?" His voice was low, tender.

And when he said it like that, she believed him.

"Sorry."

SPIKE CLOSED his eyes for a moment. "Me, too. For getting you into this."

She stared at him, one emotion after the other flickering across her face. "I'm willing to shelve the issue in the interest of our mutual survival."

"Good. You can yell at me when we're back at the Hilton. Ceasefire?"

"Ceasefire." She nodded.

The wind howled outside.

"The storm is not all bad, you know," he said. "It's erasing our tracks." And although the sandstorm slowed them down, it also slowed their pursuers.

"So you're in some kind of an antiterrorist unit?"

"I understand that you're frustrated, but I can't discuss this with you."

"You dragged me into this. I want answers. Where is the rest of your team?"

He said nothing.

"So you can't tell anyone? Not even your family?"

"I don't have a family."

"None?"

"My parents immigrated to the U.S. from Sweden. Dad was a cop, killed in the line of duty when I was six." He swallowed at the memory of that night—people at the door, the crying.

"It must have been difficult for your mother to raise a young child on her own."

"Mom was the super of this run-down tenement building we lived in. One day, the power went out, which was an everyday occurrence. If two people used their hair dryers at the same time, it'd blow a fuse. She couldn't find her flashlight so she took a candle to the basement instead to see if she could fix things. Turns out, on top of the glitch in the electricity, we also had a gas leak. I was at the top of the stairs and got blown clear. She didn't make it."

Abigail's expression softened. "That's terrible."

He shrugged. He didn't need anyone's pity.

"What happened to you after that?" she asked.

"It doesn't matter."

"Well, you have to talk to me about something. You won't talk about your work."

"I was about ten. I went into foster care." There was this old Italian guy, Giuseppe, who lived in their apartment building who had wanted to adopt him. He had watched him now and then, but Social Services wouldn't go for it. They considered him too old, plus he was living on a very small retirement income.

Her eyes swam in sympathy.

He hated it. "I managed. Had some good families and some bad ones." He'd learned street fighting because of the latter. Then one day, he had defended himself too effectively against some drunk bastard who had only taken him in for the money from Social Services, which he pissed away on booze. He was sent straight to juvenile hall after that. Giuseppe had passed away by the time he'd gotten out.

"Is that why you went into the military? It must have been hard to have nowhere else to go."

"I went to college, actually." One of the counselors took him under his wing and straightened him out, helped him get scholarships. "I was good at languages." He'd supported himself by translating for a couple of agencies.

"You speak Arabic amazingly well. You must have spent a lot of time in this region."

"Some." He nodded.

"So what happened after college?"

"I got a job." At the FBI.

"I don't suppose you're going to tell me more about that?"

He shook his head.

"Have you ever looked for your relatives in Europe?"

"No."

She seemed surprised. "Why not?"

"I've never known them." His parents had made enough money to support the family, but certainly not enough for European vacations.

"Are you ever going to?"

"Probably not." He was a loner. Not because nobody wanted to hang out with him, but because he preferred superfluous relationships. He didn't get attached to people easily. And considering his work, that suited him just fine.

He didn't want the responsibility of a family. Didn't want to have his kid standing in the doorway listening to some stranger tell him his father was dead.

"So what do you do when you're not saving the world?" she asked.

"Some car racing. It's the perfect stress release. You

have to watch every second what you're doing, be in the moment one hundred percent to avoid injury. It doesn't let your brain think much about anything else."

She nodded as if she knew what he was talking about. "That's what I used to love about skiing."

He could definitely get into skiing, he thought as he looked at her. In fact, a snowy mountainside just about anywhere sounded like heaven right now. He needed a vacation. In his mind, he could see himself flying down the mountain and then relaxing in a hot tub afterward. He went absolutely still. Because in the picture conjured by his mind, Abigail was sitting in the hot tub with him.

He shook his head. No way was he going to entertain fantasies of Abigail in the hot tub or making love with her in front of the fireplace. Damn. Where had that come from?

"Are you okay?" She was looking at him, concerned.

He took a deep breath. "Fine."

She smiled and leaned against him. "I think I'll try to get some sleep."

Just what he didn't need—having Abigail nestled into his arms seconds after she had made a grand appearance in his fantasies. He was aware of every curve pressed against him, his fingers itching to touch her.

He shifted a little and sat on his hands.

NIGHT FELL by the time Abigail woke. Spike's chest rose and fell evenly under her. The air was quiet.

"The storm's gone," he said.

She stirred and tried to pull away from him, but his arms tightened around her. "Stay still."

"Shouldn't we start out?"

"We have a visitor."

Suhaib had found them! She whipped her head toward the opening of the cave, but saw only endless sand outside. Confused, she turned back to Spike.

"Next to my foot."

Her gaze settled on a length of thick rope, tightly coiled, covered with a fine dusting of sand. And then all at once, the realization hit her. She scrambled back, practically climbing onto his head to get as far away from the snake as possible.

So much for not moving, she thought, panting, when she finally stopped.

Thank God, the snake remained still.

"What is it?"

"I've been trying to decide. Could be an Egyptian cobra or a puff adder." He kept his gaze on the snake. "Or a well-fed viper. In that case we have further options: McMahon's, Palestinian, sand, saw-scaled or horned desert viper."

She was really, really beginning to hate the desert. "All those snakes live around here?"

"In this part of the world, yes, but not necessarily in this very desert. I could probably identify it if it uncoiled."

"Are we in his cave?"

"It's probably trying to get warm. The rocks hold heat longer than the sand. Snakes love caves at night."

"Now you tell me."

Some of the sand rolled off the snake as it moved.

"You're choking me," he said.

"Sorry." She relaxed her arm around his neck and watched in horror as the snake uncoiled. The four-foot monster was yellowy brown, with dark brown bars.

"Puff adder."

"Is that bad?"

"Dangerously poisonous. Could be worse, though. At least it's not an Egyptian cobra."

"Lucky us." She rolled her eyes, but then couldn't help asking, "What's the difference?"

"Cobras are deadly poisonous."

"Meaning we'll be dying a slow and painful death instead of an instant one?"

"Nobody's dying here except the snake." He turned his rifle slowly into position and then stopped.

"Not to rush you or anything, but what the hell are you waiting for?"

"A good shot. I don't want to ruin all the meat."

As if understanding the words, the snake lifted its head in protest, looked right at her and stuck his wiggling tongue out. Then it lurched forward.

She screamed at the top of her lungs.

The sound of the gun going off in the small cave was deafening.

She could barely hear Spike when he said, "Damn."

"What?" She looked at the bloody bits and pieces scattered outside, covered in sand.

"I was hoping I could just shoot the head clean off." He pushed her off his lap and out of the cave.

She was careful not to step on anything and moved back, scarcely believing her eyes when Spike began to sort through the remains.

"You're kidding, right?"

"We have to eat."

"I'm not eating this thing. And if you are, you're never kissing me again." Did she just say that?

A grin split his face as he pulled up one eyebrow and dropped the chunk of meat. "Then you do have plans of kissing me in the future, provided I give up supper?"

She swallowed. "Not exactly plans. More like, you know—I'm not counting out the possibility."

"So you got the hots for me?"

She bit her lip, but some sounds escaped from the back of her throat.

"I like it when you growl at me like that." His grin widened. "It's very sexy."

She wished she had something to throw at him, but the only items at her disposal were snake chunks. Then the thought hit her. "Are we going to starve?"

"Unlikely. People have been known to survive for as long as ten days without food. Water is our bigger problem. At these temperatures, if we run out, it's two more days after that at most."

"Thank you for that uplifting thought."

"We'll be out of here long before our water is gone."

"You think?"

"I know. Why don't you stay here while I check out what I can see from up top?"

She nodded. That made sense. She sat on an outcropping and watched as he climbed, stepping carefully from foothold to foothold, his movements not nearly as smooth and graceful as a couple of days ago. The ribs had to hurt. In fact, it was hard to believe all he was doing. She wondered how much longer he'd be able to go on like this—injured and without any sustenance. Truth was, she admired his strength, and she was only too well aware that she depended on it.

Without him, she wouldn't stand a chance of making it out alive.

And yet, there was more to it than that. She worried for him as he climbed, and not only because she depended on him. She had come to care about him, God help her. It was as ridiculous as it was twisted. He had lied to her, used her, put her life in danger, for heaven's sake. And yet…

She had to be crazy. The heat had addled her brain.

Chapter Nine

Spike scanned the horizon in vain. Damn. He'd expected to be in Tihrin by now. The flat desert was turning into an area of undulating landscape in front of them, expanses of sand alternating with strips of rockier terrain, hills and valleys carved by wind and long-ago water, which were harder to walk through with limited visibility. In the dead desert, they could see for miles and miles. Going ahead now, they wouldn't be able to tell what was behind the next hill or tall sand drift. He didn't like it. "The camp might have been farther west from the city than I thought."

Abigail switched the rifles from one shoulder to the other and rolled her neck, keeping pace with him. She hadn't complained once—not about the heat or the forced march or lack of food.

"Want to trade?" He offered the can. "This one is pretty light." They were running out of water fast.

"I'm fine. Are we lost?"

"Technically, no. We'll reach civilization sooner or

later if we head north. But if the camp was directly south of Tihrin we should be able to see—" He listened to the unmistakable sound of an approaching car. "Get down."

She threw herself to the ground at once, and he on top of her to cover her black *abayah* with his camouflage uniform. He threw a couple of handfuls of sand on top of himself for good measure.

The camels came into sight first, about two dozen or so, then the red Toyota pickup truck that herded them.

"Bedouins." He jumped up and waived his kaffiyeh at the two men in the truck's cab, yelling at them to stop.

Unfortunately, they were angled away from him and still too far to hear him over the noise of their vehicle.

"Stay down." He grabbed a rifle and shot into the air. Then he dropped the weapon and raised both hands to the sky.

The truck stopped. The Bedouins returned fire.

He stood motionless until they stopped shooting. They weren't going to hit him from that distance. Nor did they look like they were trying too hard. They were just showing him they had guns, too, and were not unprotected in case he had mischief on his mind.

The guns fell silent. The pickup moved toward them.

"This is not good, is it?" Abigail still lay on the sand behind him.

"On the contrary. We're saved. Stand up slowly."

"Is it safe?"

"They won't shoot at a woman."

Justifying his optimism, the two men lowered their rifles as soon as they saw her.

"Assalamuh alaikum," he called out a greeting as soon as they were within hearing. Peace be with you.

The pickup came to a halt.

"Walaikum assalam." And upon you peace. A man, about thirty or so, got out with rifle in hand and then after a moment of hesitation, swung it over his shoulder.

Another man, younger than the first by a handful of years at least, came around the truck. They looked enough alike that he assumed they were brothers, both wearing the colorful flowing clothing of the Bedouin. They looked him over, but averted their gazes from Abigail. He figured the decimated hem of her *abayah* showed more leg than they were comfortable with.

"We were kidnapped a couple of days ago and taken into the desert," he said. "We escaped."

The men's faces grew dark.

"Lots of evil in the southern desert these days," the older of the two said. "Come, we'll have shelter and food for you at our camp."

"Shukran." He inclined his head. Thank you. Then, ignoring the pain in his side, he jumped into the back of the pickup and helped Abigail climb up next to him.

Dust flew around them as they returned to the camels, which began to disperse. As soon as the men got the herd together again, they started off toward camp, slower than he would have liked, following the meandering animals. Night was falling when they finally reached the tents, about thirty of them, scattered on top of the sand.

An older Bedouin, wearing a white robe and kaffiyeh, a curved dagger tucked into his belt, greeted them. *"Assalamuh alaikum."*

"Walaikum assalam." Spike jumped onto the sand and helped Abigail down.

The old man showed them into one of the larger tents. *"Ahlan wa sahlan."* Rest as in your home.

He sat on a priceless Persian carpet that covered the sand and invited Spike to join him, while two women led Abigail behind a cloth that hung from the tent's ceiling, dividing it into separate rooms.

He was immediately offered food, water and coffee, and had to tell his story to Abdullah, the clan's leader, and five sons who soon gathered in the tent. They listened gravely and apologized for their countrymen's behavior. Then he was shown a place to rest, assured that he and his wife would be taken care of. And for once he slept well, in the relative safety of the camp, knowing that even if El Jafar's people found them, the Bedouins would not easily give up their guests.

He slept an hour or so and woke to the sound of drums and the smell of roasting meat. Saliva gathered in his mouth, his stomach churning with hunger. He stepped outside and drank in the sight of the camp preparing for a feast under the starlit sky. His gaze settled on Abigail next to one of the cooking fires.

She was taller than the Bedouin women, exotic in a purple *abayah* that had a line of golden patterns running down the arms and sides, a *burqa* covering her face below her eyes. She looked like a nomad princess. The drums heated his blood, and he had a sudden vision of throwing her onto the back of a fine Arabian horse and carrying her off. Which made no sense at all. What could he possibly offer her?

His one-bedroom bachelor apartment in D.C. seemed pitiful all of a sudden. And even if she was willing to go, to give up the work she was so obviously passionate about, how long would it be before his next assignment left her to wonder when and if he was coming back? He couldn't do that to her. He couldn't ask that of any woman.

He walked to the men who sat around a carpet on the sand. As soon as he took his place among them, an older woman came over with a large platter of food and placed it in the middle. Each man ate from the common platter, scooping up food from the side of the platter closest to him, some using a piece of flatbread, others their fingers. Careful to use his right hand, he did the same. But as hungry as he was, he barely tasted the food, his eyes returning over and over to Abigail. The women did not eat with the men.

"You have not been married long?" Abdullah asked.

He turned his attention to the man, embarrassed that he'd gotten caught. "A week or so."

"She is the wife of your heart." The clan leader nodded with a knowing smile.

He didn't know what to say to that.

Then someone asked him to retell his story, which had apparently circulated around camp while he slept and had aroused much amazement and speculation. He did so, saying as much as he could, rewriting the parts he could not talk about.

"It is good in the eyes of Allah to take care of the orphans and widows." Abdullah nodded in approval when he told him of Abigail's work in Tukatar. "It is different for people in the towns. They've forgotten the old ways. None here would ever go hungry as long as any of us had food. My people live or die together." A fierce pride filled his voice, pride for his people and his culture.

Other men shared their tales, too, when he was done—tales of encounters with bandits and robbers. The stories went on late into the night, some true accounts, some no more than folktales. Spike leaned back on one elbow as the old Bedouin next to him took his turn.

"I heard tell of a wealthy merchant once," he said, his eyes sparkling in the light of the fire. "He had a virtuous and comely son for his eldest, but his stepmother, wanting more power for her own sons, tried to poison him."

A couple of the men nodded, no doubt having heard the story many times before, while the young boys watched the speaker, mesmerized. Spike took a sip of his drink, as his gaze sought out Abigail once again.

"He had, however, a most magical talking horse who cautioned him. The young man ran away from home dressed as a common beggar, his horse disguised as a donkey, and they joined the sultan's service. Now, the sultan had a daughter of exceeding beauty and the young man fell deeply in love with her. But on one fateful day, raiders attacked the palace."

The boys leaned forward, drinking in the old man's words.

"The merchant's son fought like a lion against them and overcame the enemy. His true identity was then soon revealed, and in gratitude the sultan gave his daughter to him for a wife. They returned to the house of his father and had many children—"

Spike jumped up as he caught the sound that had interrupted the speaker. A few other men around the fire came to their feet, too. The rumbling of engines grew louder. Trucks. Two or three of them.

"You better stay out of sight." Abdullah nodded toward his tent and pulled his rifle closer.

The rest of the men did the same, while the women and children disappeared out of sight. Spike glanced around the tents, wondering which one Abigail had gone into. There was no time to look for her. He ran into Abdullah's. He waited inside the thick leather flap that covered the opening and listened to the voices that filtered through it.

"*Assalamuh alaikum.* We're looking for two Americans. A man and a woman. They're thieves and murderers."

He recognized Suhaib's voice.

"*Walaikum assalam.* We've seen no strangers since we set up camp here," Abdullah responded.

"I see you are having a feast."

"My youngest daughter gave birth to a son today. Come feast with us. *Ahlan wa sahlan.*"

"Thank you, but we must find the ones we seek. The foreigners are dangerous."

ABIGAIL LOOKED around the women's section of the tent, at Sara, her unwed daughters and three young sons. Sara was Abdullah's first wife, and the head wife among the four, each of whom had her own tent. She had seventeen children—twelve of them still living, she'd told Abigail proudly earlier, making her realize what an achievement that was, how much sacrifice and constant vigilance it took to keep that many children alive under the harsh conditions in which they lived.

She hated the thought that she had brought danger to them.

Indistinct voices filtered in from outside. The men were talking and not fighting—a good sign. Still, she wished Spike was there with her. She felt safer when she was with him. Then, after some time, came the sound of motors starting, the noise slowly fading away into the chatter of the women around her.

Abdullah called through the carpet that was serving as a divider, and Sara responded. She couldn't understand either of them, their Bedouin dialect beyond her Arab language skills. When Sara motioned to her to follow, she did so.

They didn't go far. She was shown to another "room," to Spike.

"There you are," he said, resting among a jumble of pillows, like some harem lord.

She pulled off the *burqa* that covered part of her face. "What happened?"

"I told Abdullah you were my sister and he asked for you for one of his sons. He's giving me a camel and enough food and water to get to Tihrin as your bride price."

For a moment she couldn't think.

"It wasn't an easy trade considering your age. Would have helped if you were thirteen or so. I had to swear on all my ancestors that you were still a virgin."

"You've got to be—" Then she saw a grin hovering over his lips, and threw a pillow at him, hard. "It's not funny. This is no time to joke."

"Relax." He reached for her hand and pulled her down next to him. "They're gone. We'll head out first thing in the morning. If we left now, it would look too suspicious."

"You have a sick sense of humor," she said, her mind still stuck on being left behind. But then she couldn't help smiling, the tension seeping from her body.

He nuzzled her cheek.

She drew back. "What are you doing?"

"They think we're newlyweds. We should probably make some kissy-kissy noises," he whispered. "My manly pride is at stake here. I don't want them to think American men neglect their wives."

"You're crazy."

"If I am, you made me so," he said and claimed her lips.

His kiss was incredibly gentle, his arms around her reassuring. He nibbled her lips playfully, licking the corner of her mouth, tasting her, testing her. He pulled back a little to rest on one elbow, and in the light of the single oil lamp next to them, she could see him smiling at her.

She was shocked by the strength of her suddenly awakened needs to have the warmth of his body cover her again, his lips back on hers. And she could tell the exact moment he read the flare of passion in her eyes. His face grew serious, his blue eyes darkened. He lowered himself and gathered her tightly against him, his lips brushing her cheeks, then her eyelids, the tip of her nose, then finally finding her mouth. She shouldn't be doing this, she thought, and kissed him back.

The world melted away as she floated in the warm sea of his caresses, weightless, careless, at peace and at the same time mindlessly aroused. It lasted forever, not nearly long enough. When he reluctantly pulled back, he took her breath with him, and her lungs, or maybe something else in her chest, leaving her aching and empty.

He lay on his pillow and gathered her close. "Sleep."

If only she could. Unfortunately, the memory of the kiss was enough to keep her up for the rest of her life. Her gaze fell on two small jars by the tent's wall. *So that's where they went.*

She sat up. "Hang on, I've got something for you."

He crooked an eyebrow.

"Not that."

"Okay." He grinned. "Because I'm trying to be a gentleman here and not push you, but if you're offering, don't expect me to turn anything down."

She swallowed. Good thing they were clear on that.

She retrieved the jars and opened the shorter one. "Abdullah's wife made this earlier for my wrists." She dipped in a finger and looked at him.

He took a deep breath and lay back on his pillow. "Treat away."

She smeared the smooth substance over his bruised face and watched as it was quickly absorbed, leaving nothing behind but a faint minty scent in the air.

"Thank you." He came up on his elbow. "My turn?"

"You don't have to. I can—"

"I want to."

He took the jar from her and spread the ointment on her wrists in gentle caresses. It felt nice, cool and tingly.

"I could kill them for doing this to you."

She looked away. "You did."

"They went too easy. I couldn't afford to make any noise. For this, I would have liked to see them suffer." He closed the jar. "What's in the other one?"

"Something for your ribs. Sara said it's good for people kicked by the camel. I think."

He opened it, sniffed the contents and made a face.

"You sure she didn't say she made it from something *dropped* by a camel?"

She caught a whiff of it then, too. Looked as if they wouldn't be sleeping snuggled together after all. Still, if it helped, it was worth the stench.

"Sit up," she said, and when he did so, she unraveled his bandages and applied the sticky substance carefully. "Does it hurt?"

"Nothing hurts as long as you're touching me."

"Stop fooling around. I'm serious."

"Me, too," he said, his gaze intent on her face.

She picked up the long strips she'd ripped from her *abayah* and tied them back one by one, her arms around him as she looped the material around his back, her face inches from his chest. She tightened the last strip and moved away.

His hand closed around her arm.

She could find no air in the tent; if there was any, it was too thick with passion to be breathed. She swayed toward him. *...if you're offering, don't expect me to turn anything down.* She couldn't do this. She couldn't start anything she wasn't sure she could stop.

She pulled away from him and settled into the pillows with her back turned. "You stink."

"Now that hurts," he said, but she could hear the smile in his voice.

ABDULLAH WOKE him before dawn. "*Sabah alkhair.*"

Spike managed to untangle his arms from around

Abigail without waking her, then got up and stepped outside their portion of the tent to where the man was waiting. "*Sabah alkhair.*" Good morning.

He followed him outside to the coffee fire, where a copper pot let forth the most fragrant steam, tantalizing his senses. They sat and he gratefully accepted the cup of spiced coffee Abdullah handed him, along with a small plate of cold meats.

"Forgive me, friend, but I cannot keep you safe," Abdullah said after a while. "Our camp is surrounded."

"I wish to bring no trouble to you or yours. We will leave at once."

The man nodded, probably relieved. His customs would not have allowed him to ask the guests to go, no matter how worried he was about his own family. "You can leave with the camel herd," he said.

"Will they let the herd go?"

"They will." He nodded, somber.

And then he understood. Suhaib's men were preparing to attack the camp. If a handful of camel herders left, that meant fewer men for them to fight. "I do not want your family to come to harm."

"*Insha'allah.* What Allah wills will happen. Don't worry. When they come, they'll find this lion is not yet without his teeth." Abdullah sipped his coffee.

"*Shukran.*" He thanked him for all he'd done and all he was about to do, putting his own family in jeopardy to save the lives of strangers.

Abdullah nodded to one of the men milling about,

and he brought a set of worn clothing, a loose robe and kaffiyeh.

Spike accepted it with more thanks. "May I have some grease, if there's any left from the feast yesterday?" They'd roasted a ewe.

Abdullah called out to one of the young girls, maybe six or seven, and she ran off behind the tent to appear within a few minutes with a shallow dish.

Perfect. He scooped some with his fingertips and rubbed it into his beard. As the girl watched him with rounded eyes, he gathered some cold ashes from the edges of the fire and rubbed that on top of the grease.

Abdullah nodded with approval. "My friend is most wise," he said. "You will go away from the city. Less suspicious. Then you can circle back. My sons will show you the direction before they leave you."

"*Shukran,*" he said again, the simple thank-you seeming far too insufficient. He stepped inside the tent, picked up two of his rifles and brought them out, laid them at the man's feet then pulled a knife from his pocket and set it on top.

"It is not necessary, my friend." The old man lifted his arm in protest.

"A humble gift. A symbol of our gratitude. We could never fully repay you for all you've done for us." And that was the truth. The man was putting his own family at risk for them.

"You must prepare." Abdullah pointed to a large

leather bag at the opening of the tent. "For her. Women don't go out with the camels."

He stood, picked up the bag and took it inside to Abigail, listening to the voices of women and children on the other side of the divider. She was dressed and ready to go, *burqa* in place. Every inch of her skin was hidden and, still, just her eyes took his breath away and brought back every memory of their kiss the night before.

"I'm afraid you'll have to travel in this." He set the bag next to an empty plate on the carpet. The women had brought her breakfast.

She nodded instead of protesting. He admired that about her, the way she always did whatever needed to be done, without thought to her own comfort, without complaint.

"Nice beard. You look good in gray."

"Very distinguished-looking, isn't it?"

"I wouldn't go that far." She ran her gaze over him, squinting her eyes.

"What?"

"Your, um, physique. It's not exactly grandfatherly."

She was right. He was taller and a lot more muscular than any of the men in the camp. He picked up a pillow. He could do nothing about his height, but he could correct his proportions. He stuffed the pillow under his robe and made sure it was held in place by his belt. "What do you think?"

"Pregnant grandmother with excessive facial hair?"

He could see she was grinning from the way her eyes crinkled.

"I was going more for the well-fed wise old man look, you know—the tribe elders and all."

"You'll do fine." She stepped into the bag and sat first, then lay down and curled on her side.

He closed the top, careful to leave plenty of opening for air, and then lifted the bag.

"Are you sure this is going to work?" Her voice was muffled.

"Don't worry. I'm not going to let anything happen to my precious cargo."

Two camels were waiting for him in front of the tent by the time he stepped outside the opening flap. One of the animals had a matching bag already hanging from his other side.

"Food, water and a small tent." Abdullah gestured to the bag.

They hung the bag with Abigail in it to balance the first, but when he moved to get on the camel, Abdullah pointed him to the other one.

He was giving them both camels? With the food, tent and clothes, they were receiving a considerable gift. The clan was not a rich one.

"*Shukran,*" he said, humbled by the man's generosity once again. "I wish I had something to repay you."

"It is pleasing to Allah when his children share his blessings" was Abdullah's only response. He patted the camel's neck and it stood.

To her credit, Abigail stayed quiet and still.

He climbed on the back of the other animal and once it got on its feet, he headed toward the rest of the herd, leading Abigail's camel on a rope.

"Ma'assalama," Abdullah called after them. Go in peace.

"Alla Isalmak."

The men moved the herd out at once. They had barely left the camp when the army Jeep pulled up alongside them, the man in the passenger seat yelling to Abdullah's sons and asking them about strangers. They denied having seen any. The Jeep moved forward.

Spike pretended to be busy untangling the reins when they came in line with him. He kept his gaze on the task, not sure if they could see the color of his eyes in the semidarkness. But it seemed his person did not draw their attention; the bags did.

One of the men yelled at him to stop. He kept the camel going. The man stood in the back of the moving Jeep and lifted his rifle. Spike shifted in the saddle getting ready to grab for his own gun.

The man turned his weapon and smashed its butt into the bag. The tent inside shifted, a corner peeking through the bag's mouth, which the strike busted open. The Jeep pulled forward, leaving them literally in the dust.

"They're gone," he said to his saddle, careful not to turn toward the bag that held Abigail, and watched as the Jeep circled back toward Abdullah's camp.

They had gained some time, but not much. Abdullah's resistance would slow El Jafar's men but could not stop them. And once they searched the camp, they would realize their prey had escaped and would come after him and Abigail. He had to evade them long enough to reach the relative safety of the city.

HER STOMACH rolled with motion sickness from the nonstop swaying of the beast. Abigail took a deep breath then another, gagging on the combined odors of sun-baked leather and camel sweat. Her limbs ached from being crunched up for hours; her bladder was about to explode. She wasn't going to make it much longer. Safety or not, she would have to get out.

Then, just as she was about to tell Spike, the animal stopped. *Oh, thank God.* She listened, but couldn't hear anything beyond the men who had come with them. No sound of vehicles approaching, no strange voices. Dared she hope they were taking a break?

"Ready to come out?" Spike's voice sounded like that of a savior angel's from above.

"Ready, willing, but probably unable." She croaked the words through her parched throat. She had finished her water flask some time ago, drinking more and faster than she was supposed to, out of nervousness and boredom. Her stretching bladder and crackling lips were the direct result.

Her stomach rolled again as the camel swayed and lay down. Then the flaps of the bag opened and she had to close her eyes against the bright light. She tried to scramble out, every movement a prickle of pain.

"Hang on," Spike said.

She felt his strong arms scooping her up, lifting her. He held her in his arms, showing no intention of letting her go. She blinked, squinted her eyes to look at him.

"Thanks."

"My pleasure." He lowered her feet slowly onto the sand.

Her knees buckled as she tried to put her weight on them, but he held her up with one arm, massaging her shoulders with his other hand as they waited for feeling to return to her legs.

"Better?" he asked when she could finally hold her own weight. But he didn't let her go.

"Much."

"Are you gonna be okay on your own for a minute?"

She nodded.

"Sit here." He helped her to the spot shaded by her camel, and handed her the ropes of both animals before walking off toward Abdullah's sons.

True to his word, he was back in no time, carrying a dagger, its handle ornately carved. "A parting gift," he said.

She glanced over at her camel, at the men who were moving out the herd, then back at Spike. He set the weapons down and unstrapped the empty bag from her animal. She rose to help.

"Take a break," he said as he took the pillow from

under his shirt and tossed it onto the sand, shedding several sizes miraculously at once. "Stretch your muscles." He took the ropes from her.

Right. Great idea. She did need to stretch her legs. All the way to the nearest Porta Potti. She headed for the closest sand dune with painful, shuffling steps.

"Where are you going?"

"To the bathroom?"

He shook his head. "I don't want you out of sight. You can go behind the camels."

He tied the camels to the full bag, using it for an anchor, and walked away a short distance, scanning the terrain, picking up rocks here and there. She appreciated the effort he made to give her privacy and squatted behind his camel, the larger of the two. Two giant eyes looked at her.

Great. "I can't do it if you're watching."

The camel snorted.

"Fine." She turned around. She was used to the lack of indoor plumbing, had gotten over her sensibilities during her trip to Uganda. For a moment, she thought of the dense bushes with wistfulness. Not much privacy in the open desert. The only thing she asked for was no onlookers. She took a deep breath. She was not going to get hung up on one peeping camel.

She stood when she was done, and felt good enough to really look around for the first time since they'd stopped. Abdullah's sons were nowhere in sight. Spike was a good fifty feet away with his back to her, still examining the terrain. They were alone in the desert once again, in some kind of a wadi, an ancient dried-up river bed. Scraggly yellow-brown grasses peeked in scattered tufts from the sand; a handful of nearly leafless trees rose like admonishing fingers, not one over five feet high.

"What do we do next?" she called out to him.

He glanced over his shoulder, then turned and walked back to her. "We make camp."

"Do we have time?"

"No. But if we don't stay out of the noon sun, we'll be going nowhere. We can't help anyone if we're not alive." He grabbed the camels' ropes, got them standing, walked them to one of the dead trees and tied them up.

She opened the tent bag and got out a rolled-up carpet, woven wool panels enough for a small tent, and a bundle of food. Then she carried them to the remains of the other tree.

Spike came over when he was done with the camels. He helped her to secure the top of the panels to the trunk and fanned out the bottoms, anchoring them with stone and stand. The end result was as ugly as it was flimsy, but they only needed it for a few hours, and it did provide the necessary shade.

He grabbed their food and water and carried it inside. She looked around at the empty desert, expecting as she had all day the sound of trucks, the terrorists popping up from behind one of the sand dunes. Nothing. They might just make it. She tried to make herself believe that as she stepped through the opening after Spike. He held the leather flap open for her and let it fall after she passed, closing them in. Not much room, but plenty of light to see. The sun was bright enough to filter through the panels.

She took off the *abayah*, her veil and *burqa*. As much as the thin cloth in front of her mouth had bothered her when she'd first put it on, she'd come to appreciate its advantages. It kept the sun off most of her face and neck, and the sand away from her mouth. A definite plus out in the desert. The pants and long thin dress Sara had given her felt soft against her skin. She was grateful to the woman for having given her a gift of fresh clothes.

Spike put their food—smoked meat, goat cheese, flatbread and dried figs—in the middle of the carpet. "Let's eat. Then you can rest."

"I'd just as soon rest first." She hated motion sickness. She was no longer dizzy, but her stomach was far from ready for food.

He lifted the waterskin for her. "Drink at least. A few bites of flatbread probably wouldn't hurt, either. You might feel better if your stomach is not empty."

She swallowed some water while he moved closer and felt her forehead.

"Does your head hurt?"

"No." Thank God. She didn't need to feel any crappier than she did already. She reached for the bread.

"You could have gotten heatstroke." He examined her face. "We should have stopped earlier."

He'd told her at the beginning to let him know if she began to feel sick, or too hot, or needed a break for whatever reason. But she hadn't wanted to slow them down. She had figured she could handle it. And she *had* handled it.

"A few minutes is all I need." She closed her eyes.

The heat itself was exhausting. She wondered if she would ever get used to it, if she'd ever be fully functional like the Bedouins or the people of Tukatar.

"Take as long as you want," Spike said, and settled down next to her.

And for the first time, his presence, his overwhelming body so close to hers, comforted rather than rattled her. But still, it was a long time before she could relax. The thought of a group of terrorists combing the desert for them, hunting them, circled in her exhausted mind. The race was nearly at an end, the winner still unclear.

Time was running out. By now El Jafar's men had figured out that they weren't in Abdullah's camp. Their pursuers would know they were heading for Tihrin, the nearest city where they could hide and make connections. The terrorists had trucks that would catch up with the camels easily. And they were coming after them. If she and Spike could count on one thing, they could count on that.

Would they reach the safety of the city or would the terrorists reach them first?

Chapter Ten

The brief rest helped; so did not having to go back into the bag. Abigail wiped her forehead as she scanned the horizon. The swaying didn't bother her now that she was on top of the animal, breathing fresh air. She urged the camel to go faster. They had to get to Tihrin. Their lives and the lives of thousands depended on it.

Thank God, they were pretty close now. For the first time she felt a glimmer of hope. Maybe, just maybe—

She heard the approaching vehicle before she saw it. An army truck.

"Get down behind the camel." Spike was already making his animal lie down.

She stopped her beast and slid onto the sand, tugged on the rope until the camel kneeled then went down all the way. Trying to flee would have been futile. They couldn't outrun a truck.

Spike handed her the rough-braided rope of his animal and lifted his rifle over the saddle. "It's them. They must have split up to search for us."

He was probably right. No other vehicles were visible on the horizon. She recognized the truck, with the right front mashed up and the headlight missing, the home-dyed canvas half blown off. She spotted only two men, both in the cab, none in the truck bed.

Spike aimed and missed. Both men returned fire immediately. The camels bolted to their feet. She struggled to hold them, the ropes biting into her palm. One of them was slipping, but she had to hang on. Losing the animals would be a death sentence. And yet the rope slipped again. She could not hold both. Spike's, the stronger of the two, broke free and took off in a panicked run. She managed to hang on to the other one, but could not make it stop and lie down again. The animal halted for a second; then, as more bullets flew by them, it rushed forth again. She dug in her heels and succeeded, but only for a moment. The camel lurched forward. She tripped, nearly lost that rope, too, as the camel dragged her across the sand.

Then Spike was there and got hold of the rope, jerked it hard enough for the camel to pay attention. "Get down."

A second passed before she realized he was talking to her. She dropped on her stomach. The truck was closing the distance fast. Spike was on one knee, pulling the camel down. *Oh, my God.* She stared at his right hand, covered in blood.

For an agonizing moment her heart stopped, as did the world around her. Then she blinked, shut everything from her mind but what she had to do. "Are you hit anywhere else?"

"No." He handed her the rope as he fumbled with the gun. "We have to take them before they radio in our position. The others can't be far."

"Let me try." She reached for the weapon.

"I want you to stay down."

"I can do it."

"I know." He still hesitated, but when she tugged on the rifle, he let it go and took the rope back. "The sight is off."

She took a couple of deep breaths. *Steady.* She waited for the calm, and it came just as it always had during the competitions. Nothing existed but the gun's sight and her aim. She aimed for the driver's head and shot out the lonely headlight, corrected on the next shot, aiming a little above, a little to the right, and squeezed the trigger. The man slumped forward; the truck abruptly changed direction. There was a break in firing as the other man took control of the wheel.

She aimed again, trying to compensate for the air that shimmered from heat and made her work harder yet. She got him on the first shot. The truck slowed then stopped.

"Not bad." Spike's expression held approval and maybe even admiration.

It felt nice. "I told you I could do it." She set the gun down, her hands trembling again.

"It's not that I didn't think you could. It's that I hate

to see you in harm's way. Is that too chauvinistic?" He flashed her a disarming smile.

She could feel her lips tug up in response. "It's kind of sweet in an old-fashioned way. God knows, most of the time I need all the help I can get. Just not when it comes to guns."

"I can see that." He picked up the rifle. "I'm going over there to check them out. "You stay here and don't let go of that camel."

That was fine with her. It was one thing to do target shooting, aiming for the middle of the bull's-eye; it was entirely another to shoot at a person, even if in self-defense. She was not prepared to inspect the results. Instead, she scanned the desert for anybody else and found nothing but Spike's camel, an increasingly smaller dot on the endless sand as it raced away from them.

Spike was back in minutes, driving the truck, the broken windshield knocked out. "Get in."

She climbed up and slid onto the seat, turning her head from the smudges of blood on the dashboard, grateful that he had cleaned up the rest. Her gaze settled on the radio, riddled with bullet holes. Spike must have hit it.

He got out, loaded their bags in the back and smacked her camel on the rump, sending it on its way.

"Are they going to be all right?" she asked once he was back in the cab.

"They should be able to find their way back to camp."

He was probably right. The camel walked straight in the direction from which they'd come.

"How is your hand?"

He started up the truck and stepped on the gas.

"Nothing serious." He held it out for her inspection as the vehicle picked up speed.

It didn't look as if he'd taken a direct hit. More likely, his skin got ripped when the bullet hit the rifle and jerked it from his grasp. There was some skin missing, and he had probably pulled some tendons pretty good.

"Feeling is coming back to it now." He made a fist and then relaxed his fingers.

"You should let me take care of it."

"We're not stopping for a while."

With their waterskin in the back, there was no way to wash the wound without stopping.

"Let me at least wrap it up so more sand doesn't get into the wound."

He grinned. "I like it when you're worried about me. It shows that you care."

She tore a strip from the bottom of her brand-new dress under the *abayah*. "I'm only trying to keep you around because I don't know how to drive a stick shift."

"Sure, babe." He grinned even wider. "Whatever you say."

EL JAFAR roared with frustration. How was it possible that the Americans had not been captured yet? They were two foreigners in the desert his men knew like the back of their hands.

With every passing hour, the chance of their reaching a town grew. He could not afford that.

"Today!" he yelled into the cell phone. "Put every man on it. I want every car out looking."

Anger filled him, rage that pressed hard against his temples. He would not be thwarted. His fate was to change the world his people lived in, to return his country to greatness. He would fulfill that fate, and all who tried to stand in his way would perish.

"The next report I want from you is that they're dead," he said, his voice calmer now and cold.

Then he closed the phone and hurled it across the room, watching with satisfaction as it smashed into pieces against the stone wall. Shards of black plastic littered the Persian carpet, along with bits and pieces of wire. Soon his enemies would be crushed liked that. With his own hands he would bring vengeance.

Pain, fire and death.

He could already taste the sweet zest of victory. He could see how it would be, the shift of power across the continents. And his people—the whole world, once it understood his foresight and courage—would have him to thank.

The two half-dead Americans running for their lives in the desert could not, would not, stand in the way of that. He would make sure of it.

ABIGAIL STRETCHED her aching back. They didn't stop to rest until they were well into the night, deciding to sit out the darkest part of it. The truck had no headlights and they didn't want to risk flipping it over on a sand dune.

She spread the tent panels in the back of the truck for extra cushioning and rolled out the carpet on top of them. There were no trees around, nothing to use as poles to set up the tent properly. They didn't really need it, anyhow. The truck kept them elevated, away from any poisonous snakes and scorpions in the sand. They could have stretched the canvas of the truck overhead, but instead, Spike had taken it off. Probably so no one could sneak up on them.

The night wasn't exactly balmy, but it was comfortable enough to sleep, the air standing still. She unpacked their food while Spike refilled the gas tank from the cans they had found in the back. For once, they had lucked out. They had plenty of gasoline to make it out of the desert. Spike had made sure of it before he'd let the camel go.

"Supper is ready." She sat down on the carpet, her legs folded.

Spike came up, wincing as he hoisted himself over the side. His ribs were probably still hurting. His face looked slightly better though; the swelling had gone down. He'd cleaned the grease and ashes out of his beard, and a few drops of water still glistening here and there.

He gave her a wide grin. "Honey, I'm home."

She blinked.

He sat across from her and grabbed for the food.

"Let me take care of your hand first." She unplugged their waterskin; when he put down the smoked lamb chop, she scooted over to him.

He held his arm out over the side of the truck, and she pulled off the dirty, bloody cloth and then poured as much water on his hand as she dared, wishing for some kind of antiseptic. She plugged the waterskin tight and set it aside, then ripped another strip from the dress Sara had given her to wear under the *abayah*.

"This should help some." She bandaged the torn skin without once looking up into his eyes and moved away as soon as she was done.

He picked up the meat again, but after a moment set it down. "What's wrong?"

She reached for a dried fig, a slow ache building in her heart. "Nothing."

Except that she was in the back of a rusty old truck in the middle of the desert, pursued by crazed terrorists, and she finally had found the man she could actually imagine saying, "Honey, I'm home," to her on a regular basis. And of course, he wasn't available. When this adventure was over—if they survived it—he would disappear and she would never see him again. She didn't even know his real name.

She looked up and found his gaze on her.

"You look beautiful in the moonlight."

Her breath caught, but then she gathered herself.

"You know you've been too long without a woman when you start thinking of me as beautiful."

She was not ugly, but no one would mistake her for a cover model. She didn't have swollen pouty lips and high cheekbones. Nor could she manage anything that remotely resembled a smoldering gaze.

He wiped his mouth with the back of his hand. "There are all kinds of beauty."

"Stop depressing me. The surest sign that you're unattractive is when other people tell you that there are all kinds of beauty."

"Stop talking yourself down."

He was right. She shrugged. "When a major relationship goes under, it has a way of shaking one's self-confidence."

"What happened?"

"He betrayed me." Let Spike make of that what he wanted. She certainly wasn't going to detail how she'd gotten a call from some doctor's office asking for Anthony, wanting to follow up on some procedure. When she questioned the nurse, the woman wouldn't tell her more than that. God, she had been frantic with worry. She'd thought he was sick, wanting to spare her by keeping it a secret. And when she couldn't take it any longer and told him about the call, he finally admitted he had a vasectomy—knowing how much she wanted children. He didn't, he'd told her when it was too late for discussion. Apparently, he hadn't wanted to argue about it, so he'd gone and taken care of it behind her back.

Such manipulation and dishonesty she could not forgive. “He lied to me,” she said.

“Someday he’s going to regret it.”

“He already does.” According to her mother.

They ate in silence for a while. She put away the leftover food when they were done.

“Are you going back to him when your project is finished?”

She busied herself with their packs, wishing he’d drop the subject. “No.”

Her relationship with Anthony seemed as if it had been a thousand years ago. The childish crush she’d had on him in the beginning had long faded; she’d been just too busy performing to expectations to notice it. She had almost married him because everybody had always expected that she would. And because she’d felt she had to make up for the fact that her sister, Kate, couldn’t marry and have a family. Not because she had been truly in love. The message from the doctor’s office had been a last-minute wakeup call.

“No. I’m no longer mad at him, but it’s over. I’m not going back.”

“Good,” he said right behind her. “Then I won’t have to feel guilty about kissing you.”

His lips touched her cheek as his arms wound around her and he slowly turned her in his arms. Then his mouth found hers.

His gentle caresses alone were enough to drive her mad. Never would she have thought a simple kiss could be so powerful, could take hold of her so completely. He tasted like the mint tea she'd brewed earlier in the sun. His arms around her felt familiar, right, safe.

He sank to the carpet and pulled her with him. She went willingly, lost in the magic that swirled thick around them every time they touched. Her breasts ached for him as he caressed them through her clothes. Impatient, she drew the *abayah* over her head. And still, he wasn't close enough. She reached for the hem of her dress.

He put his hands over hers and stilled them. "Are you sure?" His face was inches from hers, his gaze intent, his self-control visibly strained.

Wasn't he? She pulled back feeling rebuked and looked away.

He cupped her cheek to make her look at him. "I want you. All of you or as much as you're willing to give. I just want to make sure that you understand that this is it. This is all it can ever be."

She understood well what he was saying. Once they were out of the desert, he'd be gone. There'd be no picket fences. She slipped her dress over her head, sitting there half-naked in the moonlight, her one and only bra left in the Harebs' guest room.

"I shouldn't be doing this," he said even as he reached for her, his voice low and raspy. "You're driving me crazy."

"I want to," she whispered, floating away on the waves of sensation sent across her skin by his touch.

"Drive me crazy?" he murmured to the spot of skin between her breasts.

"I want to do this with you," she said as she buried her fingers in his hair.

With a low, rumbling sound of desire, he rolled with her until she was pinned under him, his lips a hair-breadth from hers.

"I'm going to make love to you, Dr. DiMatteo."

She sneaked her hands under his robe, and her fingers glided over his well-muscled chest. His body, his strength awed her. He was without a doubt the most attractive man she'd ever seen. And there was so much more to him than that.

She gasped as he pressed the unmistakable proof of his desire against her, then gasped again as his lips found her nipples. While his mouth was busy driving her mad with need, his hands freed her from her pants and underwear. Then he pulled away to look his fill.

"You are beautiful," he whispered and lifted his gaze to hers. "Do you doubt me?" He reached for her hand and laid it on top of his hardness.

Her fingers curled around him instinctually, and he closed his eyes for a moment. Then he opened them again and lowered his mouth to hers.

"Still, beauty I could resist," he whispered against her lips. "But you're brave, too." He nibbled her lower lip. "And compassionate." He moved on to the corner of her mouth. "And intelligent." He licked the seam of her lips. "And strong."

She opened her mouth in response, and he claimed her fully. Her head swam from his words as much as from his touch, her thoughts jumbled. But then again, who needed to think when his hand was drawing lazy circles on her abdomen, spiraling down? Then he was there and cupped her mound, the heat of his palm sending delicious shivers through her.

She moaned into his mouth and felt him grin.

A seeking finger buried itself in her hair, then another parted her feverish flesh. Brooks bubbled, birds sang, somebody was playing a harp in the background, or maybe it was a violin. A whole orchestra of violins.

He moved a fingertip back and forth slowly over the spot that ached for him most, his palm massaging her. Then another finger found its way to her opening and pushed inside, stroking, pressing in and out.

She looked up at the starlit sky as his lips moved from one nipple to another and back again, her hands gripping his shoulders to stop from falling into the abyss that stood before her. And then she stumbled, in bursts and constricting muscles and pulsating palpitations.

He rolled her on top of him and held her tightly.

An eternity passed before she could talk. "What about you?"

"I have a breathtaking naked woman in my arms. I'm happy."

He was hard under her. And despite his assurances, she couldn't help investigate whether she could make him happier yet. She rubbed against him.

"Vixen." He grinned and captured her lips.

But she wouldn't let him keep her captive long. She

trailed kisses down his chest, making a detour for his flat nipples, reveling in his low groan of desire. She moved to his belly button then lower, pulling his pants and underwear down little by little as she kissed each newly revealed inch in turn.

Impatient, he kicked his clothes off, and then he was naked in all his glory. If braying camels fell from the sky, they could not have made her look away.

"I want to feel you inside me so much it hurts."

He hauled her up. "You're killing me." He kissed her soundly and flipped her over, rubbing his hardness along the cleft of her buttocks. She squirmed, drowning in mindless passion as he slipped a hand under her and found her again.

She was ready, on the edge. She turned to face him and reached for him, ran her fingers along his length. His eyelids lowered. She closed her hands around him and moved them. He lowered his head for a kiss and moved against her.

"You're making my knees shake." He laughed and fell on the carpet beside her, turned on his side and pulled her to him face-to-face. He claimed her lips one last time, then pulled away.

She could see in his eyes what it cost him. He was holding back for her sake. Didn't he know how much she needed him? They've been staring death in the face for so long now, and it wasn't over yet. If they didn't make it out of the desert... She wanted to make love with the man she—she didn't dare finish the thought.

Instead, she went to him, with him when he turned on his back, and she ended up lying on top. Her knees bent on their own, bringing her up. Her gaze not leaving his face, she straddled him, gaining satisfaction from the way his eyes darkened.

He swallowed hard.

"Unless you don't want to…" She held her breath.

"More than life itself," he said.

She lifted and sheathed his hardness, her head falling back, her spine arching, as mind-numbing pleasure seared through her body.

His thumb found her. She moved.

Nothing had ever felt this good.

She was blowing in a windstorm of passion like a grain of sand. The storm grew and grew, inside her, around her, threatening to rip her apart. But when it crested, it left behind not destruction, but endless pleasure. They clung to each other in the night.

"Wow," she said when she could finally speak.

"Ditto." Spike's voice sounded raspy. "Mint tea. Who would have thought?" He hugged her tighter.

"Or some strange desert atmospheric conditions."

"Huh?"

"Don't pay any attention to me. I've been sexed mindless."

"Me, too."

She smiled against his cheek, too tired to open her eyes.

"I've never seen stars look as beautiful as they do in the desert," he said after a while.

She rolled on her back and looked up. Magnificent. Then again, it was possible that she was just a little bit biased. After all, she'd just had the best sex of her life.

SHE AWOKE ALONE, but saw him in the cab of the truck as soon as she turned her head. He was playing with the radio.

She was still naked. Memories of the night rushed her and took her breath away all over again. Never had she been more thoroughly made love to. It had been certainly different than anything she'd shared with Anthony—his quick, perfunctory caresses and hurried couplings. She'd used to leave her underwear on one leg so she wouldn't have to go looking for it afterward. She glanced around, but couldn't see her undies anywhere. Her lips stretched into a smile of pure satisfaction.

Spike had made her feel like a woman. More than that, he'd made her feel sexy, passionate, desirable. And beyond the physical—the thought scared her for a moment. But yes, there were things that went beyond the physical between them, even if only on her part. He was going to break her heart when he left.

She sat up and ran her fingers through her hair. She would have given anything for a comb and toothbrush. She pulled on her clothes and took a swig from the flask of mint tea, rinsing the taste of sleep from her mouth. Time to pack up. She dressed, found her panties after all, then stood to roll up their blankets, the carpet and the tent.

She turned at the sound of the truck door opening. Spike came up over the side.

"Good morning." He drew her to him and thoroughly kissed her. "You ready?" He didn't pull back far.

Oh yeah. Definitely ready. Too bad he meant ready to hit the road. She nodded.

"About last night..."

God, here came the part when he said he was sorry they got carried away.

"It was the best night of my life," he said, and she felt her face split into a giant grin. "But we didn't use any—"

She touched a finger to her left arm. "I have an implant." She needed it to regulate her cycle.

He nodded. "I don't want you to worry. Where I work... We get tested regularly for everything."

She thought about the AIDS test she had to take before she could be approved to work with the children. But as she opened her mouth to reassure him, she heard the trucks. A bunch of them this time.

"Let's go." Spike jumped over the side then helped her to the sand.

They were in the cab within seconds, the motor coughing to life. Spike slammed his foot on the gas.

"Do you think they found those two I—"

Her question died unspoken as she heard the first gunshots flying over the sand. They reached the top of the next big sand dune, and there lay the city before them with its skyscrapers and minarets, shopping centers and mosques. And police. The army even, most likely. Even now that the war had been long over, they were still stationed in major cities to keep the peace.

Just a couple of miles now. They were saved. In the crowds of the city, they were sure to lose the men who hunted them. Abigail took turns looking forward and back, judging the distance to safety, the distance between themselves and the angry men behind them.

Ahead stretched tracks in the sand that turned into a gravel road after a mile, then into a paved street flanked by shanties as it snaked toward the city. Soon they reached the outskirts, their pursuers still behind them, although their guns had disappeared from sight.

Spike wove in and out of traffic, narrowly avoiding a donkey cart, braking hard for running children, as he merged in with the jumble of vehicles on the road. The terrorists were about ten cars behind them, still coming.

The farther they got into the city, the more clogged traffic became. A few of El Jafar's men hopped off the trucks and blended into the crowd of people on the sidewalks, moving forward.

"We're stuck." She scanned the road as far ahead as she could see. The cars rolled forth with lazy ignorance of the desperate situation behind them.

"See that alley?" Spike pointed to a narrow passageway between two restaurants on her side of the road. "When I stop the car, run for it as fast as you can. I'll be right behind you."

She barely had time to think before the motor died. She pushed the door open and jumped to the ground. Horns beeped behind them. She didn't look back as she made her way to the sidewalk across three lanes of traffic and plunged into the mass of people, where she disappeared among the women, all dressed the same.

Her heart raced, but she reached the alleyway and stepped into its darkness.

"Run," Spike said next to her ear, startling her.

He didn't have his rifle, too long to be concealed. Although coming and going fully armed was common in the country, it would have drawn instant attention in Tihrin.

The alleyway ended in a smaller side street. Spike took the lead, crossing through a store, hurrying up another street, ducking into another alley, all the while moving rapidly farther into the city, until they reached a square of shops.

"Stay here." He stepped into the square, leaving her in the shadow of a palm tree.

He went into one of the stores, came out, went into another and another. Then he was back.

"Let's go." He led the way to a restaurant straight ahead.

He asked to be seated on the upper floor and then chose a table near the door that led to the roof.

"Do you think we lost them?"

"We'll see." He kept an eye on the square. "I called for backup."

"From one of the stores?"

"I told them I'd been robbed and needed to place a call to the hotel to send us a car. The first two shopkeepers were suspicious and wouldn't let me in the back office to use the phone, but I lucked out with the third."

A waiter brought them cold drinks then walked away. Her heart still beat at about a million beats per minute. She scanned the street from the window. A lot of people went about their business, none of them acting as if they were looking for someone. She glanced at Spike, who was paging through the menu as if he hadn't a care in the world.

"So when is the backup coming?"

"Soon. There's a U.S. Air Force base just on the other side of the border, about thirty miles from here."

The waiter came back to take their orders.

"We've been robbed and have no money with us," Spike told him. "Would it be possible to send a bill to our hotel? We're staying at the Hilton."

"One moment, sir." The man walked away.

He was back within minutes with the manager who apologized for the lack of public safety on the streets of his beloved city, expressed hope that the visitors were not terribly inconvenienced and assured them that their meal would be entirely on the house.

"Are you okay?" Spike asked after they'd placed their order and were finally alone again.

"A little shaken, but none the worse for the wear. You?"

"Been a hell of a lot worse, that's for sure."

She nodded. He did seem to move easier. Sara's ointments worked wonders. Or maybe their bodies understood this was no time to fail, or even to slow down.

He held her gaze, his face serious. "About us. When this is over—"

She held up her hand to stop him. She didn't want false promises. When this was over, they were over. There was no future for them together. She'd known it all along. She'd go back to Tukatar and he would disappear. No need to complicate things now. Which was why she made a point of not asking his real name. She had a feeling that when they parted, she would be asked to forget they had ever met.

She could never do that, would never forget him. But she was a bigger person than to lay on the guilt, to make him feel like he owed her something because of the amazing night they had spent together. She had gone into this with her eyes wide-open. She was a big girl. She could handle it. Her heart wouldn't be the first in history to be broken.

He nodded, as if understanding her silent message. "You might be questioned. They kept me in the same cell the whole time, but you were moved around. You might have seen something. In any case, you saw more than I did."

"Of course." Whatever it took to capture those men and stop their plans, she would willingly do. "You'll be going back, then?"

"Yes." His gaze was somber.

"Be careful."

A large platter of food was brought out and set between them on the table, cutting off whatever response he was going to give. They ate in silence, his gaze straying to her over and over again. She refused to cry.

"If things were different—" he said.

"I'm fine."

He smiled. "I hate it when you're so damned brave. And it definitely bugs my ego when you're tougher than me."

She couldn't help smiling back. "Suck it up, soldier."

Chapter Eleven

The sand turned into rocky terrain as they rode for the border. Abigail stared at an enormous boulder through the tinted windows of the black SUV that had picked them up. The driver, a distinguished-looking Arab man in his midforties, slowed for the border guards.

"I don't have any papers." God, she hadn't even thought about that. Her passport, along with everything else she had, had burned with her hut.

Spike turned back from the front passenger seat. "You're fine. Nothing to worry about."

The car stopped, the driver rolled his window down and flashed his ID at the guard. She waited for the soldier to ask for the rest of their papers, but he didn't so much as look at them. He stepped back and waved them through.

Right. She was playing with the big boys now. God, what had she gotten herself into? She glanced back, at the soldiers and Beharrain behind them. Tukatar and the kids seemed unreal now. She had been picked up and swirled around by the winds of fate—and dropped at another location. But she could not forget the kids, what she came to Beharrain to do. They still needed her. No matter what came next, she would find a way back.

"Almost there," the driver said in perfect, unaccented English, speaking for the first time since he'd picked them up.

She turned back to the road in front of them. Spike had been right about the Air Force base. It sprawled just a few miles ahead.

Security was heavier than at the border, the gate well-guarded, but once again, they passed through with ease. The driver wove his way around marching soldiers and military vehicles, then stopped in front of one of the smaller buildings. He got out and opened her door. And a soldier was already there waiting for her. Where had he come from?

"This way, ma'am," he said with a Texas twang. He was young and tall, with the reddest hair she'd ever seen.

She looked back at Spike. He was deep in conversation with an older man in civilian clothing. He glanced up and caught her gaze. "I'll find you before I leave," he said to her and then turned back to the man.

She could do nothing but nod, move forward. Then she was through the door and led down a long hallway. To the infirmary, she realized, when the double doors in front of her opened. She was ushered into a spacious room with beds lined against the wall, IV stands next to them, the air thick with the unmistakable smell of disinfectant. The unit was empty save for a middle-aged gentleman in green scrubs and a nurse.

"We've been expecting you, Dr. DiMatteo. I'm Dr. Taylor, this is Jenny. How are you?"

"Pretty good, all considered."

He gave her a warm smile. "Hop onto this examining table and we'll check you out."

She did as he'd asked and held out her arm to the nurse, who was coming over with the blood pressure cuff.

"Any pain anywhere?" Dr. Taylor examined the fading bruises on her wrists.

"A couple of places that are tender to the touch, but nothing bad."

"Where are you from?"

"New Jersey."

"No kidding? Me, too. Where in Jersey?"

"Cherry Hill."

"My wife loves that mall."

She grinned. "So does my mother." She spent more time there than a teenager.

"One-thirty over eighty." The nurse stepped away.

"Let me listen to your heart." Dr. Taylor put his stethoscope in his ears. "All's well there," he said after a while. "Why don't you go through that door to the bathroom, give us a urine sample, then change into one of the gowns in there? I'd like to take a look at the rest of you. I promise nothing I'll do will hurt a bit."

She followed his instructions.

"Care to tell me what happened?" he asked once she was back on the examining table again.

"They started to give me electric shocks, but I passed out almost right away. It could have been worse. I think they knew I didn't have any information and were just messing me up to make Spike talk."

"Were you sexually assaulted?" His voice was somber, the look on his face sympathetic.

"No." Thank God, she was spared at least that.

"Very good." His smile returned. "I don't see anything that would require medical attention. You're a little dehydrated, but nothing serious. If you'd like, we could put an IV in, or you can just lie down here in this nice cool room for a while and have a couple of drinks."

"That would be fine."

"You can get dressed. Jenny will take care of you. It was nice to meet you. You're a brave young woman." He shook her hand before he left.

Jenny handed her two soft hospital gowns to replace the paper one they had used for the examination. "First rest a little and drink a few glasses of liquids. Then I'll show you to the showers and get you some clean clothes. I'm sure that would make you feel better."

Just thinking about a nice long shower made her feel better. "Thank you." She went back to the bathroom to change.

A man was waiting for her when she came out, Jenny nowhere in sight. He wore a black suit, his sunglasses in his hand. He looked like he walked out of the movie *Men In Black.* He was African-American, but the similarity to Will Smith ended there. This guy was a good two hundred pounds, serious as heart disease, with a shaved head that reflected the fluorescent lights. She half expected him to pull some gadget from his inner pocket, flash it in her eyes and erase El Jafar and Spike from her memory. Sure would have made her life easier.

"Lawrence Jenkins. I work for the United States government. I have a few questions to ask you," he said instead.

She shook his hand, self-conscious of her clothes, although Jenny had given her two gowns and she'd put on one to open in the back, the other to open in the front, to make sure she was covered all around. "I'd be happy to help any way I can."

He pointed her to one of the beds. The bedside table held a large pitcher of clear liquid and a glass. "I'm to make sure you rest and have plenty to drink," he said. "I understand you went through quite an ordeal."

She sat on the bed and poured.

He remained standing, although there was a chair behind him. "I wish I could give you more time to rest, but we cannot afford to waste a single minute."

"It's okay. I understand. I want to help."

"Thank you." He nodded and sat finally. "How long have you known Jamal Hareb and how well?"

She answered honestly with as much detail as she

could, her head beginning to spin after a while as Jenkins moved on from one question to the next, scribbling notes, sometimes asking the same thing again, reworded, as if trying to trip her.

They moved on from her relationship with Jamal to her work, to what she'd seen at the Hareb home, at the camp, how many men, what kind of weapons. The questions went on and on. Jenkins even had her draw a rough sketch of the buildings.

"I'm sorry." She set down the pencil at last. "That's the best I can do. I was too nervous at the time to pay attention to details."

"You're doing fine. You weren't trained for this."

"If I saw it again, I could probably point out the building where the main headquarters are. I'm just not sure how many other buildings stood between it and the trailer Spike was held in."

"You've been very helpful, Dr. DiMatteo."

"As long as you find the camp, you can neutralize them, right? I mean drop a bomb on the whole thing or something?"

"Unfortunately, that won't work this time. They have a significant weapon that we can't risk setting off. We'll have to go in. That's why knowing who'll be where and what to expect is extremely important."

"Are you from the CIA?"

"I work for the government," he said unblinking.

"I believe I was going to be recruited. Could we not still do that? Then I could go with you and point out the buildings and what I remember of them." Did she just say that? Did she just offer to go back into that hellhole instead of running screaming in the opposite direction? What was wrong with her?

Spike. He was going back—into unspeakable danger. If there was a chance she could help him, she would take any risk to do it.

Jenkins shook his head. "We should have satellite pictures in another half hour. You can look at those and tell me what's inside the buildings. That should be sufficient."

SHE WAS WEARING army fatigues, sleeping. Spike bent over to smooth the hair out of her face. "Hey, babe. Ready to roll?"

Her eyes fluttered open, her gaze unfocused for a second before settling on his freshly shaved face. Her lips stretched into a smile.

"Not in the hay, unfortunately," he said. "The choppers are ready."

She sat up so suddenly, their heads nearly collided. "I'm going?"

"I was told you volunteered. You sure?"

"Yes."

"They asked me for an evaluation…" He dragged out the words, teasing her.

She was wide awake now. "And?"

"I told them you could handle it. The satellite pictures were worthless. What wasn't already obscured by the camouflage overhead had been covered by the sandstorm. We'll identify as many targets from the air as possible, then the chopper is going to drop the team in. You'll be brought back here right away, before the first shot is fired."

"I'm going." She grinned. "Thanks for the vote of confidence."

"They asked me if you were capable and I told them the truth. But if you're asking whether I want you to go, the answer is hell, no."

Her smile widened, her kissable lips drawing his gaze.

He swallowed. "I wish we didn't have to hurry."

She looked great in pants, all legs. He stood, not trusting himself to sit on her bed. The small distance didn't help any. And then he held out a hand to help her up and her touch made things worse. He pulled her close and kissed her, long and slow, then pulled away and leaned his forehead against hers.

"I'm going to make sure nothing happens to you."

"I know."

He wished he felt as calm. He wished they didn't need her. He wished she had refused to go. Funny, he couldn't picture her doing that. She always stood up to whatever challenge came her way. He loved that about her.

"Come on, then." He led the way outside.

The rest of the team was already in the chopper, nine men he trusted with his life and more importantly, with

Abigail's. The other five Black Hawks each carried eleven men of the Air Force Elite. He bent to avoid the spinning rotor blades, and she followed his example as if she'd been doing this all her life. He helped her inside the bird and got in after her.

They had barely sat down before the pilot lifted off, the noise of the chopper overpowering everything. He was having major second thoughts about bringing her.

She leaned over and pressed her lips to his ears. "What's so funny?"

He looked at her, confused, but then caught the amused smirks on some of the guys. "I made some statements in the past about never getting married." She'd told the investigating agent everything and word had gotten around fast.

She grinned. "Sorry I ruined your reputation."

He grinned back. "I'm never going to get any respect again."

Thompson elbowed J.D. across from him and said something. All he caught was "lovebirds." Oh yeah, it would be a long time before he lived this one down. Not that the idea of marriage seemed so wrong now. He might have been rash in making a judgment before. He could imagine spending more time with Abigail. A lot more. But in his case, that was highly unlikely, marriage, in general, being completely out of the question. He didn't have the kind of life conducive to setting down roots. By this time tomorrow, he might be on another continent.

Abigail squirmed on her seat next to him. He gave her a reassuring smile and then put on his full combat gear—forty pounds worth of bulletproof vest, weapons and a gas mask. They felt like hell in that heat, not to mention the pain of the extra weight on his broken ribs. He'd been given the option of staying in the chopper and giving instructions from above, but he'd refused it. At least he'd been in the camp before. No way was he going to let Thompson, J.D. and the others go in without him.

He scanned the ground and saw something straight ahead. He patted the pilot on the shoulder and pointed. "There."

They flew over the well-camouflaged compound, the individual buildings barely visible under the giant netting. The chopper lowered to get a closer view. Much better.

"I was in that one." Abigail showed him a larger cement building with a flat roof. "You were in the trailer. I think El Jafar's quarters are over there. That's where they took me to see him."

For questioning, she meant. His hands fisted by his side as he nodded.

The sound of helicopters brought men rushing from the buildings and then running back in. A handful of shots were fired.

He nodded to the team and they stood, ready for rapid rope descent. The chopper pulled off to the side. They couldn't drop onto the netting and risk getting entangled. The ropes went down. He hooked onto one.

"Stay down," he told Abigail. He kissed her hard on the mouth, not caring who saw them or what they thought. Then he jumped.

"YOU CAN SIT up front." The pilot was patting the seat next to him.

Abigail clambered over as they pulled up and away. He handed her a headset and she put it on, watching in horror as all hell erupted below.

"Can we stay?"

"Sorry, ma'am, my orders are to take you to safety immediately after the drop."

The other choppers joined in the fight. She stared back, her heart clamoring in her chest as she watched Spike run toward the buildings. He was under heavy fire. Then the chopper turned and she could no longer see him.

"Relax," the pilot said. "Those guys are good. I'll be coming back to pick them up in no time."

She nodded, wanting desperately to believe it was that simple.

"So you're a civilian?"

"Yes." She didn't feel like making small talk while Spike was risking his life. "Can I listen in on the radio?"

"Sure." He set the dial to the right channel.

The chopper instantly filled with the sounds of people yelling all at once. Orders being barked out. Gunfire. Then Spike's voice. "Fall back, fall back." A small explosion, more gunfire. Her limbs began to shake.

Strange how she hadn't really been nervous until now. And she was nowhere near the action.

"Probably sounds worse than it is." He gave her a reassuring smile. "Want me to turn it back off?"

She nodded.

Below them, a covered army truck moved across the sand, toward the terrorist camp.

"Not ours," the pilot said and radioed the information to Spike's team.

He gave off a warning shot, but the vehicle didn't stop. Then a corner of the canvas was pulled aside on the back and the strangest-looking weapon appeared.

"Grenade launcher." The pilot took an evasive maneuver, but it was too late. The weapon was fired and the next second the chopper jerked back.

"Hang on. We're going down," he said.

She gripped the seat, fought her rising panic. The pilot tried to control their fall, but only partially succeeded. The ground was coming closer and closer, rushing toward her. They hit with a bone-jarring impact. Then there was nothing but darkness and silence.

SHE WENT to hell and the devil was trying to shake her soul out. Abigail opened her eyes and realized the shaking came from the truck moving at a good pace. She lay on the bottom between the terrorists' feet.

One of the men noticed she was awake and spat on her. "American whore," he said, his face cold with hatred.

"Let her be." The voice came from behind her.

She twisted her neck. Jamal. She scanned the rest of the truck. "Where is the pilot?"

"He didn't make it." Jamal's dark eyes shone like stone, the expression on his face hard. "You shouldn't have come to Beharrain."

"I came to help."

"Us or the U.S. military?"

"The children. Whatever else happened, I came to help the children."

"I'm sorry, then, that this is how things turned out." He looked away from her.

"It's not too late."

He didn't respond.

"Where are we going?" she asked.

"To retrieve something precious. Rest. You are our ticket out of here now. I can't have you die yet."

She squeezed her eyes shut. They were probably going to use her as a hostage to get out of the country. She tried to move a little and bit back a groan. Every bone in her body felt broken. At least she could wiggle her fingers and toes, which meant she most likely didn't have a spinal injury.

They rode for about half an hour before the truck came to a stop. The men got out, all but the one who'd been ordered by Jamal to guard her.

She had to get away. She eyed the man who sat too far away from her to even attempt to grab his rifle. And yet this was her best chance. He was only one man—

once the others returned, it would be too late. If she could somehow get away from him and get behind the wheel of the truck… It was her only chance.

She moaned and whispered a couple of unintelligible words and hoped he would come closer. He didn't move. She could hear the men shouting outside. She didn't have much time. She curled on her side, then tried to grab for the wooden bench and pull herself to her knees. Pain shot through her leg.

The men were there then, up in the truck. They grabbed her roughly and carried her out of the vehicle. For the first time, she had a chance to see where they were—in the middle of the desert somewhere. Two buildings stood in front of her, completely buried in sand, only their doors visible. Secret bunkers. From above they would look like sand dunes.

Both of them had their doors open; Jamal's men were pushing a small airplane from the bigger one. Her heart beat faster. She was hauled to the plane and dumped in the back. Pain and more pain. She fought dizziness and nausea, watching from the window as the men prepared the aircraft for takeoff. Where was Jamal? She looked at the smaller building, pretty sure she knew what they were going to bring out. Some kind of weapon of mass destruction.

A strange sound began, then grew. She watched the building's open door. No, the sound wasn't coming from there. It came from above. A chopper, she recognized at last, and then she saw it, too—a Black Hawk.

Men shot at the helicopter, rifles blazing, everyone running around. A couple were going for the back of the truck. They got the grenade launcher, fired and missed. Someone in the chopper returned fire, taking out both of the men.

What if they hit the airplane to make sure nobody took off in it? She tried to get out, but couldn't. She was in the back, the doors in the front. She would have had to climb over the front seats. Unfortunately, she couldn't move.

SPIKE SCANNED the drop zone for any sign of Abigail. "Shoot only if you're sure of your target. Dr. DiMatteo is down there somewhere." At least, he hoped she was.

They had found the pilot of the downed chopper; he hadn't survived the crash. Spike had just about gone mad when they couldn't find Abigail. The tire tracks in the sand told the story. And led them here.

He gave the signal. Ropes went over the side. He dropped, took up position back to back with the rest of his team once they were on the ground, waited for the last man to touch down. Then they spread out to find cover.

She was alive. He refused to consider the alternative. If she hadn't survived the crash, they would have had no reason to take her.

He checked out the back of the truck. Nothing but the bodies of the two men who'd operated the grenade launcher. Somebody was shooting at him from behind the door of the larger building. He returned fire, aiming carefully, and took the man down.

Why weren't they bringing Abigail out to negotiate? They had a hostage. Why not use her? Unless, of course, she'd survived the crash, was picked up by the terrorists, but then hadn't made it through her injuries. They wouldn't have killed her at this stage of the game, he was pretty sure of that. They had little leverage. She was a valuable bargaining chip. But not their only one.

He swore, trying to figure out where they kept the bomb. It hadn't been at the camp. The fight there had been over fast, and their search turned up nothing. The rest of the team was still going through the place, leaving no grain of sand uninspected, questioning the men they had captured.

But now that he had seen these bunkers, he was pretty sure the bomb was somewhere here.

He kept low to the ground and, ducking bullets, ran to the cover of the plane, then inside the larger building. No gunshots had come from there. A quick scan confirmed that it was empty, nothing but an airplane hangar.

The terrorists had lost three men, as far as he could tell. They'd now withdrawn into the smaller building, defending the entrance. He figured there couldn't be more than a dozen of them. The small truck couldn't have carried more.

It was a bad situation. The terrorists were trapped with nothing to lose. He expected them to bargain with

Abigail's life first and then, if that didn't work, bargain with the bomb. They would want to save the bomb if possible, although if that was the only option left to them, they would probably detonate it rather than surrender.

And that could not happen. Everyone in the immediate vicinity would die. And Tihrin was too close, the wind blowing in the wrong direction. A dirty bomb would cause untold damage in a densely populated area. Worse, a crisis would set political factions against each other once again. And if it came out that U.S. military was somehow in the middle of this, World War Three would begin.

He had to get into that bunker and take control of the situation, and he had to do it now.

He stepped from his cover, gun blazing, and rushed the entrance. There were four men down there, two still standing. Then one, and then the way was clear. He entered, giving his eyes a few seconds to adjust to the semidarkness. Werner, Thompson and J.D. came in behind him.

The single room was small, seven by eight or so, a staircase in the middle, leading down. He could see nothing below. He snapped on his night-vision goggles. Better. Silently, he moved ahead, watching for anything suspicious.

He reached the landing. It connected to a long corridor ahead. Empty. There were two doors on each side, all of them closed. He stopped by the first. When the guys moved into a protective position around him, he kicked the door in.

It was a laboratory, complete with workbenches, containers of chemicals, burners, books and a jumble of lab equipment. He moved forward with caution to make sure no one hid behind the desks. All clear. He signaled to the others and they moved on.

The second room was some kind of a communication center, also empty. He kicked in the door of the third. Someone was firing at them. He jumped back into the cover of the wall and signaled to the others to hold their fire. They had to be close to the bomb.

The light came on in the room. He took off his night-vision equipment.

"Come on in, gentlemen."

He recognized Jamal's voice and, after a moment of hesitation, stepped forward.

Jamal stood by a large crate, his gun aimed at the door. "Mr. Thornton. I should have known."

Spike's gaze settled on the crate. A small plastic bomb was attached to the side; he could see the numbers on the timer from the door. Nineteen forty-two, nineteen forty-one, nineteen forty…

"Where is Abigail?"

Jamal blinked. "You shouldn't have brought her into this. Only an American coward would try to hide behind a woman."

Spike had trouble sucking air into his lungs. She was dead. And it was his fault.

Jamal squeezed off a shot at him. Spike ducked on reflex. By the time he came up, the man had disappeared through the back door.

He wanted to rush after him, to kill the son of a bitch. But if they didn't disarm the bomb, none of it would matter. "I need an explosives expert."

J.D. shook his head. "Bomb squad is still at the camp."

"Get them on the radio." He swore. "Go get him." He nodded toward the back door and walked up to the crate as the others rushed after Jamal.

Fifteen minutes and thirty seconds left. He set down his gun and swore again. It had to be a bomb. He sucked at disarming bombs. That was how he'd gotten his head split open in the first place and been saddled with his nickname.

He took in the crate, wedged the blade of his knife carefully under one nail head, then another, until he worked a board loose. If by some miracle the crate did not contain what he thought it did, he could walk away and let the plastic blow. He reached in, pushed aside the packaging material.

Damn.

He drew back and squatted by the crate, blocked the rage and grief from his mind, focusing on the wires in front of him. All three were red. He didn't have a clue which one to pull. It was a funky homemade job. The bomb was small, but enough to set off the larger one in the crate. If he had more time, he could have gotten the big bomb out of the packaging and made it up to the surface with it before the TNT exploded down below. But he didn't have twenty minutes. He had nine and a half.

He took out his knife, separated the wires. Everything he had ever learned about bombs rushed through his brain, flashes of memory from his FBI training, then the more intensive SDDU course. He had barely passed them. Truth was, he was scared of explosions. His hands shook. He swallowed. He had thought he was past this.

He checked everything methodically, what connected to what, and weighed his options. If he could pry the thing off the crate and take it into another room—he pressed his face against the wood to see behind the small explosive device, used the tip of his knife to gently lift the edge. It didn't seem to move. What if there was a sensor of some sort? No, the piece didn't look professional enough for that. Did he dare to bet his life on it? He took a deep breath and pulled harder. And then he could see.

A blue wire came out back, through a hole into the wood, back via another hole and into the black box that housed the timer. An instant trigger, no doubt. He had less than a minute left. Where the hell was the bomb squad?

He had to cut one of the red wires on the front. The right one. Now. He checked the connections again. The middle wire. He rested the tip of his knife against it. God help them all if he was wrong.

Chapter Twelve

It'd been a while since the last gunshot. Abigail ignored the pulsating pain in her legs and pushed herself up enough to see out the window. At first, she didn't see anyone, but then spotted a U.S. soldier coming out of the hangar. They'd won. She was safe. Her limbs began to shake as the tension left her body. More soldiers exited the hangar and hurried through the door of the smaller building. Spike wasn't among them.

Something moved in the sand. She blinked. There. Again. A trapdoor opened slowly, then Jamal emerged, running straight for the plane. He was spotted, but too late. He returned fire; then the door of the plane flew open and he dived in, shooting back with one hand while starting the engine with the other.

He hadn't seen her. She had kept down. If he managed to get airborne, she was as good as dead. The men below were going to shoot that plane straight out of the sky.

With all the strength she had left, she lunged forward and threw her weight on him, smashing his head against the dashboard. She heard the sickening snap of a bone, wasn't sure if it was his or hers. Her momentum carried her forward and she slid out the open door, fell onto the sand in a searing explosion of pain.

SPIKE LEANED against the wall, breathing hard, and pulled off his helmet, tossing it aside. The counter showed thirty-two seconds left, and it stayed there. He'd done it. He felt a flash of relief. Then the next thought assailed him—Abigail was gone. There had been no explosion, and yet his heart had been ripped from his chest. Every thought, every emotion he had blocked out so he would be able to focus on the bomb rushed him now. He staggered under the weight.

His face was drenched, a strange thing in the desert where sweat usually evaporated as fast as it formed. He wiped the moisture from his cheeks with the back of his hand. It wasn't sweat after all. He was crying. Damn. He didn't cry. He hadn't cried since his mother died.

"Yo, Spike." Thompson rushed through the door and stopped in his tracks when he saw the numbers on the timepiece, relaxing as he realized they weren't moving. "Everything okay down here?"

Spike wiped his face again then nodded.

"We've got them. Both El Jafar and your 'wife.'"

He jumped to his feet, blood rushing to his head, not from the movement but from the sudden jolt of hope. "Is she alive?"

"I don't know. Just got the word."

He pushed by Thompson and ran down the hallway, up the stairs, out into the blinding light of the sun. He could hardly see anything, but moved toward the group of men by the plane. Then he could finally make out the motionless figure on the sand. Abigail.

He ran the last couple of yards, fell on his knees by her side. Her eyes were open but unfocused.

"She's not responding. Both legs are broken from what I can tell. Might have some internal injuries, too," J.D. said.

Werner and Erickson were already coming with a stretcher.

He held her hand. "Abigail?"

She didn't seem to hear him.

He helped the others carry her to the chopper, reluctant to let her go. "Take her now. Call in for another transport for us."

The pilot nodded. The rotor blades started up. Spike squeezed her hand one last time, then bent his head and ran back to the buildings with the rest of his team. They had a dirty bomb they had to get out of the country before the Beharrainian military came to check out the gunfire. If they got their hands on the bomb, the U.S. might as well kiss the most important piece of evidence goodbye.

They needed the bomb so they could trace it to those who had helped make it. El Jafar had been the buyer, the delivery boy. They had to find the source and take it out. Their work was far from over. He looked up at the disappearing chopper, then stepped through the smaller bunker's door.

ABIGAIL AWOKE in a white room, alone. A hospital room. She followed the line from the IV bag to her arm. Both of her legs were in casts. She hurt like hell all over. She turned her head, saw the Call button and pushed it.

A couple of minutes went by before the nurse came. Jenny.

"Hello, Dr. DiMatteo. I'm so glad you're awake." She gave her a warm smile and glanced at her vital signs on the display screen. "Let me get Dr. Taylor. He can give you an update on your condition."

She was gone before Abigail had a chance to say thank you.

Dr. Taylor came in after a few minutes. "Glad to see you're feeling better. Sorry I couldn't come by sooner. We have a couple of serious injuries. How are you?"

"What's wrong with me?"

"Nothing that won't heal, but you'll be probably uncomfortable for a while. Fractured fibulas in both legs—the right one I had to set, the other is not too bad. You also have a severe concussion, but that should be starting to feel better soon. It'll be a couple of months before you can walk. You'll be receiving full treatment here in the meanwhile. Courtesy of the U.S. government, I'm told."

"I see." She tried to think, but the pain and the pounding in her head were too distracting.

"There's a gentleman here to see you. He's been waiting for you to come to. Is it okay if I send him in?"

Spike. A mix of emotions swept through her. "Yes. Please."

"I'll check in later. If you're in pain just push that button. It's all set up with the proper dosage."

That sounded pretty good right about now. But first she wanted to speak to Spike and wanted a clear head for that. "Thank you."

The doctor nodded and left, but the man walking in a few minutes later dressed in an impeccable black suit wasn't the one she'd expected.

"How are you, Dr. DiMatteo?" The agent who had questioned her during her first visit to the base now seemed to be in a softer mood. He pulled up a chair to sit by her side, and she remembered his name at last—Jenkins.

"Fine, thank you," she said, her spirits sinking.

"We're going to make sure that you get the best of care."

"Dr. Taylor told me."

"Will you be going back to the U.S. when you're released?"

It seemed the sanest thing to do, but she had no wish

for it. Nothing had changed. The children still needed her. "I'll be returning to Tukatar."

The man hesitated. "I see."

He must have thought she was crazy. He was probably right. "Is there anyway I could talk to Spike? Gerald Thornton?"

He looked her straight in the eye. "I'm sorry. There's no person by that name on this base."

"He was at the takedown, blond—" Then she understood. Spike was already gone. She swallowed the fresh wave of pain. "Were there any U.S. casualties?"

"You were kidnapped by bandits and taken into the desert, then luckily rescued. You have seen no terrorists, no U.S. military personnel—you're just happy you're still alive, and are too traumatized by the experience to want to talk about it." He watched her face for a few seconds and added, "No U.S. casualty."

She drew a deep, ragged breath and felt her lungs fill properly for the first time in a long while. "What about my husband? He was with me when we left the village. I'll be asked."

Jenkins's expression softened. "As far as the villagers are concerned, he's been unlucky. As of now, consider yourself a widow."

She blinked, not wanting to cry in front of him.

"Do you have any questions?"

She shook her head.

"Thank you for your cooperation, Dr. DiMatteo. It's very much appreciated."

She nodded and squeezed her eyes shut, not opening them again until he was gone. Spike had left, on to his next adventure. God, she had terrible judgment when it came to men. First Anthony, who'd broken her trust, and now Spike. He'd broken her heart.

She had no one but herself to blame. He'd made no promises, just the opposite. He had let her know from the beginning that everything between them was strictly temporary.

And it was exactly that—temporary insanity.

She had a feeling that recovering from him might be harder and take longer than recovering from her physical injuries. But she would do it. She had to. Others were depending on her. She would not let them down.

ABIGAIL LOOKED after the boys as they ran out of the schoolhouse into the sunshine, each going to their chores. They worked in the mornings, took schooling during the hottest part of the day and then were back again helping the locals in the evening. Their blankets were rolled up neatly by the wall, waiting for them to return to the schoolhouse at night to sleep.

She still had trouble believing that they had a schoolhouse. Her jaw had dropped when she'd first seen it three months ago as she arrived back to Tukatar. In contrast to her fears that the boys had dispersed and she would have to start all over again, they'd all been there and then some. Grinning with excitement, they had told her how a few weeks before, a truckload of U.S. soldiers had arrived and put up the schoolhouse and the teacher's hut in a single day before leaving.

She had her hut back. With a real door.

Since the schoolhouse lent prestige to the village, the mullah had been pleased. The villagers rallied around her, convinced by the changes and feeling sorry over the loss of her husband. Small gifts arrived, an old blanket here and there, another water jug. Nothing terribly valuable, but each item needed and infinitely useful.

She used her grant money for books and food. Some of the farmers began to pay the boys in produce for their help, so food was becoming less and less of an issue. Seeing her dreams slowly become reality felt surreal and humbling at the same time. She had so many plans to take things even further, help even more people, she scarcely knew where to start.

Keeping busy had been her salvation. It kept her mind from other things that brought nothing but heartache, kept her from dwelling on the one hole in her life that would never be filled.

She put away the chalk and dusted off her hands.

"Have I ever told you about this fantasy I had about Mrs. Mootsky in the third grade?"

The familiar voice startled her. She swallowed the wave of exhilaration mixed with panic that rose inside, turned around slowly.

Spike stood in the doorway, his wide shoulders silhouetted in the sunlight. He was tall and handsome, a dream. She'd forgotten how good-looking he was without bruises. All the feelings she'd ever had for him rushed her—respect, admiration, love. Yes, love. Still there, stronger than ever. Nothing had changed in her heart. Unfortunately, nothing changed on the outside, either. They were still who they were, with no possibility of a happy ending between them. He shouldn't have come. She wasn't sure she would survive having her heart broken again.

"Hi." She didn't step closer.

"Sorry I didn't come sooner." He walked toward her. "I've been away. There was this situation I was sent to bring under control."

"That's okay. You don't owe me an explanation."

"I do." He was just a few feet from her now. "They told me you made a full recovery."

"Good as new. Are you here on another mission?" She glanced away and back, aware of him—his eyes, his smile, his scent. His presence tingled across her skin. "Sorry, you probably can't tell me. It's okay."

"I'm here on leave."

Her heart raced ahead. Hearts were foolish that way—they never seemed to run out of hope, not even when it led them tumbling into ruin.

"I missed you." He stopped within arm's reach.

She stepped back. She couldn't look at him. Her gaze settled on his hands as they reached for her. "Please, don't." Her voice came out weak, a plea.

He moved forward and took her hand, rubbing his

thumb over her fingers. "I had a lot of time to think. And I—truth is, I don't think I can make it through the rest of my life without you."

Deep inside, wariness mixed with surprise. She did look at him then, but could no longer see him from the tears pooling in her eyes. Two fat drops rolled down her face.

He brushed them away with the back of his hand. "Abigail?"

"You want the impossible," she said, wishing it weren't so. Then self-preservation kicked in and she pulled away. "It could never work, don't you see? We'd just end up hurting each other. We can't have a normal relationship. There's no sense in torturing each other." She had to be sensible, sane. Having him walk out of her life once nearly stole the soul out of her. She couldn't go through that again.

He took her hands back, pressed them together gently and kissed them. "Do you want normal?"

Of course. Didn't she? Didn't everyone? But then, why was she here, instead of living in the suburbs somewhere, planting geraniums in front of a picket fence? No. She didn't want normal. She wanted to make a difference. She wanted to do whatever that took.

Like him.

She shook her head, her tears spilling over again.

He smiled and melted her heart. "Thank God. Because I don't have any 'normal.' I only have this."

He pulled her to him and held her tightly, kissed her

eyes, her cheeks, her lips. And, at last, she was home. As long as she was in his arms, she was home, no matter if in a makeshift schoolhouse in the Middle East, or in the desert, or in the U.S. She was home when she was with him.

"I can't offer you big family dinners at grandma's dining room table," he said. "The best I can offer is sharing my meal-ready-to-eat packages over a campfire. Do you have any idea how bad those MREs taste?"

"My family does big dinners. We can always visit them if you get in the mood for crazy."

"Actually, right now I'm dying to get you alone someplace where kids don't walk in and out without notice," he said.

She smiled. Though she was still trying to process that he was back and what it all meant, she followed him outside across the short distance to her hut. His duffel bag was leaning against the wall. He picked it up and brought it inside.

"How long are you staying?" she asked as she closed the door behind them.

"As long as I can."

And that was how it would always be. But was that enough? She searched his eyes. His arms sneaked around her waist. And she could see it—a life that included him. Yes, it was enough. It was more than she had hoped for in her wildest dreams.

"It's a tough job. I won't be doing it forever. I'm thinking another couple of years, maybe. Then you'll probably be kicking me out of the house or hut or tent or whatever, telling me to get a hobby because I'm getting on your nerves." He grinned wide.

That sounded like heaven. She brushed her lips against his. He didn't need more of an invitation than that. He kissed her gently, with the promise of many years of tenderness to come.

"There's only one thing I ask," he said when, after a long time, they pulled apart.

She lifted her eyebrows, not trusting herself to speak.

"Next time we're in the U.S. together, I want us to get married again. I want you to forget Gerald Thornton. I want you to be Mrs. Jack Logan."

"Is that a proposal?" She smiled, filled with boundless joy.

"It's a direct command." He schooled his face into a semblance of a serious expression. "Technically, since I was supposed to be your recruiter, I outrank you."

"Aye, aye, sir." She laughed and threw her arms around his neck.

"Good." His eyes darkened as he lowered his head. "I hate having to deal with insubordination. It's always such a mess."

"I'd never be so brazen," she teased him.

"You're the most brazen woman I know," he said, and claimed her lips.

And it was as if the floodgates had broken open. Urgency washed over them both. He caught her as they tumbled onto her mattress, awash in mindless passion.

He covered every inch of her face in kisses, then her neck, before lifting the *abayah* over her head, followed by her dress and pants.

"I liked it better when you were going without a bra," he said as he freed her from it. His hot, wet tongue on her nipple sent ripples of pleasure through her body.

"I'm not that attached to the practice." She gasped out the words. "I could let it go."

"Good." He suckled on the nipple gently at first, then with more power. "You have no idea how many sleepless nights I spent fantasizing about this."

It was good to know she wasn't the only one pathetically turning and tossing with insomnia week after week. "How many?"

"Every single one since I saw you last."

She voiced her deepest fear. "I thought you forgot about me."

He moved up to look into her eyes, his gaze intense. "How could I forget my heart?"

Her breath caught in her throat at his words, as the rich timbre of his voice poured over her. She drank it up like fresh water, dying of thirst after having been lost in the desert of his absence forever. "I wasn't sure I'd ever see you again."

He pulled back a little, his expression growing somber. "After we got you back to the Air Force base, I was there when you came out of surgery. You were all bandaged up, bruised, white as death. And the only thing I could think of was how much better off you would have been if you'd never met me." He swallowed. "Truth is, I could have come back sooner. It damn near drove me crazy not to. I know your life would be better without me. A hell of a lot easier, that's for sure—"

"No, never say that." She put her palms on each side of his face. "Don't ever think it."

His lips stretched into a rueful grin. "How many times did you have to face mortal danger before you met me?"

What kind of a question was that? "When I was in Uganda I had heatstroke."

"Okay, so once in your entire life."

She wanted to tell him that it didn't matter, but he put a finger over her lips to silence her.

"Do you realize that while we were together, your life was in danger at least once a day? The bandits, the firebomb, the Hareb house, the terrorist camp. Should I go on?"

"It was hardly your fault that the bandits attacked us on the way home from Rahmara."

"If I didn't manipulate you into having to marry me, you wouldn't have had to go to Rahmara."

She needed a moment to process that. "You wanted us to get married?"

"I wanted you in a situation where you couldn't simply walk away from me or tell me you weren't doing the documentary and send me home. I knew you would have no other choice once I spent the night."

It seemed like a million years ago. "I don't care."

"How can you not care? I lied to you every step of the way, I manipulated you, I put your life at risk. Can you forgive all that?"

"I'm not saying I wasn't mad when I first figured it out, but I was there at the camp. I know why you did what you did. I don't know what I would have done given the same situation. Perhaps I would have done the same."

He searched her face. "And if I have to leave and can't tell you why, if I go missing for months at a time, can you live with that?"

"I'll have to. Because I know I can't live without you." She pulled his head down to her.

He kissed her with a fierceness that took her breath away. Then after the first crushing wave of passion, he slowed, tasted her more leisurely, explored her body with his hands. His lips moved down her chin, her neck, between her breasts, looping around them in concentric circles until he found one nipple, then the other.

She arched her back, pleasure shooting through her, heat gathering between her legs, need building, tension tightening. He kissed a trail down her belly, around her belly button, then lower. His fingers parted her flesh and opened her most secret part to his tongue. She moaned his name.

He licked, nibbled, laved. He brought her to the edge then sent her over in extravagant fireworks of pleasure until she lay before him depleted, her bones feeling soft, as if melted.

"I love you. I want to spend the rest of my life with you," he murmured against her lips.

"I love you, too." She kissed him.

And then he entered her, moving forward slowly, inch by inch, driving her mad, filling her all the way. She lifted her hips and began to move against him. His eyelids lowered. She felt the pressure build, higher and higher, until they soared together in the sky.

An eternity passed before they came down and lay spent in each other's arms. Then slowly, she became aware of an odd noise coming from the roof, the sound of a flock of birds pecking. No, not birds. Rain.

"I've heard of people making the earth move when they make love, but us," Spike murmured as he nuzzled her hair, "we opened the heavens."

Yeah. She smiled. They sure did.

Epilogue

Spike pulled on the rope, making sure the palm branches were on tight. Almost done. From the ladder he was standing on, he could see the dozen or so new huts in what the people of Tukatar were calling the youth quarter. The people were proud of their growing village. The huts, built for the older boys who now came regularly to Abigail for schooling, were to give them a start in life. With a home, eventually they could hope to attain a wife. No father would give his daughter to a man without property.

The thought of this many new families starting, the lives Abigail's project would turn around, filled him with pride for his wife. She had only been here a year and look what she had accomplished. She was really something. Sometimes he wondered what on earth he'd done to deserve her, but he was happy as hell she thought he did.

He reached for the next branch, whistling. The walkie-talkie crackled in his pocket so he picked that up instead.

"I think the baby is coming." Abigail's voice came through with a fair amount of static.

He almost dropped the walkie-talkie. "Are you sure?"

"I can feel the head." She sounded somewhat tart.

"Uh—" Panic filled him so swiftly and completely, he wasn't sure he could climb off the ladder. Then his muscles went on autopilot and he moved faster than he had ever moved before, barely registering the curious glances his mad rush elicited.

"Am I too late?" He flew through the door, barely catching a glimpse of her panting, her face covered in sweat, before the outraged midwives pushed him out.

He went straight to the window. "I should have taken you back to the States."

"I'm fine," she said, sounding fairly normal.

The contraction must have passed. He searched his brain for all the things he'd learned from reading *What to Expect When You're Expecting* three times, but his mind had gone blank. Thank God for the midwives.

He paced, unable to stay still. "You should have called as soon as it started."

Her response was a deep groan.

He peeked in the window, but couldn't see anything past the women. Then Abigail screamed. Oh, hell. Nothing and nobody could have kept him from her side. He made it through the door just in time to see the baby's head slip out and stood rooted to the spot as the shoulders came free with the next push and one of the women pulled his little girl into the world.

He blinked his tears away as he knelt by their side, took Abigail's hand and kissed it. "Are you okay?"

She was smiling from ear to ear, her eyes on the small bundle in her arms. "What should we name you, my little angel?" she whispered.

"How about Kate, after your sister?"

At that, the baby opened the most beautiful blue eyes he had ever seen, and let out a squeal that attested to healthy lungs.

He laughed, his heart spilling over with joy. "I think she approves."

Abigail was smiling and crying at the same time. "I think she does." She turned to him. "I love you."

His throat constricted. "I love you, too." Then before he could kiss her, the midwives succeeded in chasing him out again, telling him that she needed rest and that they needed time to clean her and the baby up.

Stunned, that's what he was. Shell-shocked. He had a family. The best family in the world. He wouldn't have traded their little hut for all the riches of the universe. This was where he belonged.

His cell phone rang, but in his daze, the sound took a while to register. He pushed the button, mumbled a hello.

"I'm calling to let you know you should have a delivery today from the Air Force base. Your wife's family asked to get a package to you and the boys and I added a few things to it. Hope everything is going well," Colonel Wilson said.

"Thank you, sir." He was about to share his good news, but the Colonel went on.

"Good. Rodriguez said it better be a girl. His son is going to need a girlfriend in a couple years."

"It's definitely a girl, sir." The prettiest little girl ever born. His chest swelled with fatherly pride. "But you can tell Rodriguez the boy will have to get through me first."

* * * * *